Thunderhead
Part 3

This volume is the fifth in the
famous Flicka series. My Friend
Flicka appeared in two volumes,
and now Thunderhead appears in
three parts.

Thunderhead
Part 3

Mary O'Hara

Dragon

Granada Publishing Limited
Published in 1966 by Dragon Books
Frogmore, St Albans, Herts AL2 2NF
Reprinted 1973

First published in Great Britain by
Eyre & Spottiswoode
Copyright © Mary O'Hara 1944
Made and printed in Great Britain by
C. Nicholls & Company Ltd
The Philips Park Press, Manchester
Set in Intertype Plantin

Chapter Thirty

Eat something, said Nell to herself, as if she were speaking to a child. You'll feel better if you do. You must.

But she continued to stare out of the window, sitting in the armchair in her bedroom wrapped in her dark blue robe, her feet drawn under her because of the chill that filled the house. There was no fire on the hearth and the bed was not made and her hair was not brushed.

It was one of those raw October days that should be shut out by fires and curtains and cheerful voices. On some such days Nell worked furiously from dawn till dark, cleaned and mended and made new curtains and counted and took out and packed away and potted geranium slips and cleared the flower borders. And there were other days when, if she moved at all, it was to wander listlessly, pausing at every window, wondering what she had come into this room for, wondering if it was morning or afternoon – what day of the month. . . .

Gus's heavy tread was on the stairs, coming slowly. He rapped on the door.

"Come in!"

"Bring you some wood, Missus."

"Oh, I haven't used up what's here."

"You must have a fire."

"It's not very cold."

Gus kneeled down, removed some of the ashes, laid and lit the fire, and carefully brushed the hearth. As he got to his feet he threw a quick glance at Nell. Her gaze was on the fire now, the lips of her soft mouth parted. There were dark hollows under her eyes and her face looked both old and childish.

Gus started to speak, hesitated, then came out with it. "How de Boss come out mit selling de horses, Missus?"

"I don't know."

"He in de east still?"

"No. In Laramie."

"Laramie! Ven he get back?"

"I don't know exactly. But it was in the paper about a week ago."

Gus leaned to brush up a few more imaginary ashes. "You come down in kitchen, Missus. I'm getting some lunch."

"All right, Gus. Is it lunch time?"

In the warm kitchen Gus moved about efficiently and set a cup of hot strong tea on the red-checked tablecloth before her, some baked beans, well-flavoured, topped with crisp browned salt pork, and some of her own bread, toasted on top of the stove.

Sitting opposite her, stirring his tea, his pale blue eyes studied her thoughtfully. "You sick, Missus?"

6

"No, Gus."

"You going to ride dis afternoon?"

"I don't know." She looked at the food before her and took her fork in her hand, then felt her stomach shrink and close. Her belts had grown very loose these days; her slacks hung on her hips.

Gus appeared to be giving thought to nothing but the demolishing of the great pile of beans on his plate. "If you cud get a jackrabbit – de chickens needs meat –"

Nell drank a little of her tea and set the cup down. "Well – I might. Later in the afternoon."

"I saddle Gypsy for you, Missus."

Nell stirred her tea, staring a hole through the table-cloth.

"Dot Gypsy – she's wid foal."

"Yes, I know."

"Und de Boss, he don' want she should have no more foals."

"She must have been bred before he took her away from Banner last spring – early."

"Ya. Und dot mean she's foal dis winter."

Nell buttered a small piece of toast, made herself eat it.

"You don' like de beans, Missus?"

"I like them, Gus, but I'm not hungry."

She went upstairs again and slowly tidied her room, with many pauses to stand at the window. The bleak skies and the colourless world looked back at her balefully.

Later in the afternoon she put on her black woollen jodhpurs and her warm grey tweed jacket. A few strokes of the comb through her hair drew it back and she fastened it in a little bun, brushed her bang smooth and drew on her small black visored cap. As she picked up her felt-lined gloves and the red scarf for her throat she suddenly wanted to hurry and get out of that house.

The black mare galloped along, and the slim pliant

7

figure sat her with an easy, unconscious swing. Occasionally her head was flung back and the gesture was like a cry for help. Ranging around the horse were the two dogs, Kim and Chaps.

Nell was glad of the small duty to perform, the getting of meat for the chickens, was glad of the gunboot strapped under her leg. She felt as loose and rootless on the ranch as a tumbleweed.

With the passing of her lethargy her mind became painfully active. An excited argument began and she put herself first on one side of it and assured herself that there was nothing serious the matter with Rob nor between himself and her, and then she put herself on the other side and insisted frantically that it was unheard of – the way he was treating her!

Galloping along the County Road, Gypsy pricked her ears and turned her head towards the Saddle Back.

"No, you don't, old girl – we're not going up there."

Gypsy whinnied, getting the wind from the band of brood mares beyond the crest, but Nell pressed her spur against her and held her in the road.

She counted the time since Rob had left on September tenth. It was nearly a month. Figuring four days for the trip to Pennsylvania, then a week or ten days for the sale, and two days for the trip back – that would have brought it to September twenty-sixth. Where had he been since then? Laramie, apparently, just twenty-five miles away. And hadn't come home. Hadn't even written. And here it was the second week in October.

She turned Gypsy through the gate into nineteen and they galloped over the uneven ground which led down to Deer Creek. Ahead of her a migration of bluebirds rose like a cloud from the grass, then, as she halted, they descended, and each bird lit on a stalk of grass. It looked like a field of big blue flowers, and when a puff of wind

8

came and made the grasses sway, it seemed as if the blue-birds were swinging on purpose, just for the fun of it.

Nell rode slowly forward, hating to disturb them. They rose to let her through, fluttered and circled above her, then lit again behind her and continued swinging on the grass stems.

Reaching the bank of Deer Creek, Gypsy was belly-deep in dried brown grass. She grunted softly and turned her head towards the water. Nell sat relaxed in the saddle while the mare waded into the stream, her feet sinking deep in the soft gravel, and the fresh and delicious smell of water and damp earth and autumn leaves wafted up and made Nell wonder why, now, everything that was sweet sent a sharp pain through her heart.

Long wheezing sucks came from Gypsy. Two magpies were quarrelling in a tree overhead. And a little way off there was frantic yipping from Kim as he chased a rabbit. The cocker never yipped nor would he let a rabbit draw him into hopeless chase. He knew in advance where the rabbit would go and intercepted it.

Nell lifted Gypsy's head, turned her, and the mare scrambled up the bank, scattering water from her hoofs and her mouth. And as she resumed her canter, Nell resumed the argument. Rob had been in Laramie about two weeks and hadn't let her know. Why? Didn't he want to see her?

The dogs had vanished completely. Often they started out on a ride with her, were led off by rabbits or exciting scents and disappeared. She wouldn't see them again until she got home and found them panting on the terrace.

At the thought that Rob did not want to come home her mind spun around to his point of view. How was he thinking and feeling? Was he suffering too? *Oh, I hope so, I hope so, for if he loves me he couldn't help it. But does he? He could come to me, but I couldn't go to him. Or could I*? She thought of herself driving down to Laramie, going about hunting for her husband – No. *No!* She tingled with shame. She had to wait here, but how long? Yes – *how long?* Until he decided to come back. She was entirely helpless.

As these thoughts chased each other through her mind, her body and her nerves were played upon as if by little whips. Alternately hot and cold – weak, or strengthened by a wave of pride. Again and again there went through her heart and stomach a rush of sinking emptiness, and each time she recovered from it as from a shock, slowly, and weakly; a difficult comeback. It was that which prevented her from eating, for it came often just as she had prepared food for herself and sat down and looked at it.

She wondered at those mysterious physical activities, probably governed by the endocrine glands, which are the reactions to violent emotions. What, really, was going on in her body? Was it a sort of shell-shock? Was it destroying her health and strength and youth? She could not bear to look at the face that peered back at her from the mirror.

In the timber of number sixteen the dogs appeared again, madly chasing a rabbit. Up here the shaded depressions amongst the trees held snow left from a recent storm. The rabbit was in the snow, struggling towards a pile of rocks and Kim was bearing down on it, yipping hysterically.

Nell drew rein and watched the chase, quieted by a feeling of fatalism. What chance did the rabbit have? It was like her mind – doubling and dodging, trying to find a hole in which to hide, or a path of escape, but cornered every time.

The rabbit doubled on its tracks and Kim, who always went too fast, shot past it. The rabbit was struggling to

10

reach the rocks. No doubt he had a safe hideaway underneath them. Would he make it? Kim was almost upon him, and again the rabbit turned and dodged, and again Kim shot past and had to brake and turn and in those few seconds the rabbit reached his haven. But ah – Chaps was there too. The canny black cocker emerged from ambush at the last moment and seized his prey.

And then the kill. The tiny squeals of the rabbit – the sharp nosings of the dogs – the sudden jerks of their heads and snappings of their jaws.

No blame to them, thought Nell, as she galloped towards them and called to them to stand back. Wagging their tails proudly they stood off and looked up at her. They were panting, and their long red tongues hung, dripping, out of the sides of their mouths.

Nell picked up the big jack – it must have weighed six pounds – and asked Gypsy's consent to hang it on the saddle. Gypsy pricked her ears and drew in her chin, snorting. Nell offered it to her to smell. Gypsy sniffed the rabbit gingerly, and after that, permitted Nell to fasten it to the saddle.

The dogs watched her, well satisfied. They knew that later, when Gus skinned it, they would get their share.

The hunt and the killing of the rabbit had added to Nell's depression. She could not bear to go home. If she could ride until it was completely dark, and there would be nothing to do but pull off her clothes and fall into bed! If she could ride until she was so tired that she would be sure to sleep!

Occasionally she glanced upward to see if there were any stars, or if the moon was rising, but the sky was a solid grey lid, not low or stormy, but withdrawn and bitterly cold. It made her shiver. If there was beauty and life in Nature, where had it gone? When the skies were

11

like this they put a blight on the world, and on the human soul.

They galloped along in the gathering darkness, the dead rabbit thudding against the mare's side.

Nell reached the stables from the south pasture. She had expected Gus to be watching for her, but no one was there, not even the dogs. She fed Gypsy, unsaddled her and turned her out. She hung the dead rabbit in the meat house and walked slowly and unwillingly down through the Gorge. Physically, she was near collapse, and she walked slowly and unsteadily.

As she approached the house she suddenly stopped walking. Lights shone in all the windows and a row of cars stood behind it.

It was one of those uproarious gatherings which occur when town people descend on their country friends with all the "makings". The house was bursting with food and drink, lights and roaring fires and human noise and movement. Rob had brought T-bone steaks. Potatoes were already baking and Genevieve Scott was just putting the finishing touches to two big pumpkin pies.

When Nell stood in the kitchen door, dazed and almost unbelieving, and exclaimed, "Rob!" she was promptly enveloped in a rowdy bear hug by her husband, and thereafter by Rodney Scott and Charley Sargent. She was told to sit down and rest herself and let her guests do the cooking and set the table. Morton Harris brought her an old-fashioned cocktail. There would be nothing for Nell to do, they assured her, but make her famous dressing for the lettuce.

"And the mustard and coffee sauce for the steaks!" exclaimed Rob.

Gus was concocting the potent Swedish punch called *glögg*.

"And I hope," said Bess Gifford, "that there'll be room in the oven for these biscuits."

"And we'll be ready to eat at about eight-thirty," said Rob, "and until then there's nothing to do but drink up and enjoy yourself!"

Nell ran upstairs to her room. *Rob is home. He kissed me. He is here!* This very night they would be together in this room and all would be explained and forgotten. That dreadful loneliness – that desolation – it was all over. An easy breathing lifted her breast and it was new and pleasant and free and a great change – as if, all these weeks, a painful thong had bound her lungs.

She stood on the threshold of their bedroom, wondering if he had been there already, if there would be some sign, his coat thrown across the pillow, or his boots standing argumentatively in the middle of the floor. Instead, she saw the bed piled high with feminine wraps. Of course. The girls, and their things. Well – it would all wait.

Moving lightly and excitedly, she brushed and groomed and refreshed herself and ran downstairs again.

Rob offered her another cocktail. "How's about another?" he asked jovially. "You've got to catch up to the rest of us, you know."

"Have you been here long?" she asked, raising her eyes to his as she took the glass. It was like speaking to a man she hardly knew but was desperately in love with.

His eyes met hers for a split second and then fell to the glass he was handing her. "Oh, a couple of hours!" he said.

"And I'm watching you make your salad dressing!" said Morton Harris. "I've got all the things out on this table for you!"

The radio was roaring. Bess Gifford and Charley Sargent were dancing in the middle of the living-room.

It seemed to Nell she was floating on the surface of a river of sound and sensation, that lifted her higher and higher. Her body was warm and quick and pliant, the pupils of her eyes dilated, her laugh rippled. She sat at the head of the table and carved the steaks, putting a lump of butter and mustard in each slice, and a dash of black coffee and then spooning the gravy over the meat until all was blended. When, now and then, the memory of the afternoon – of all the days gone before – came back to her, she put her fork down and leaned her head back and wondered if she was drunk – so unbearably sweet was the pang of the present laid against the desolation of the past. It was over. He was here. He had kissed her. He would kiss her again tonight.

"Maybe *you'll* tell us, Nell!" shrieked Bess Gifford from the other end of the table. "Why is it that Rob and Charley are never so happy as when they can put their heads together and talk about how much money they lose on horses?"

"Lose on horses?" said Nell doubtfully, her eyes going to Rob's.

"Don't believe him," said Rodney Scott. "Come on now, Rob – give us the low-down. You made a mint on this sale, didn't you?"

"You don't have to ask him," shouted Stacy Gifford. "Take a look at him! See that smug grin! He busted the bank!"

Rob was trying to make himself heard. "If you will have it," he said, "I lost my shirt."

"That's what he was saying to Charley," insisted Bess Gifford. "And I can't see what they go on raising horses for –"

14

"Just for the fun of giving 'em away," said Charley, "or seeing 'em lose on the race track."

"Did you really, Rob?" asked Genevieve Scott.

"I did," said Rob grinning. "Who could have done it but me? I hit that sale with two car-loads of horses just when the Argentine polo players were unloading their stuff before they left the States. Their horses sold for fabulous prices. American horses sold for a song."

Nell sat very still. That was the way he had chosen to tell her. Easier on him than to tell it seriously when they were alone together. Easier on her too.

Rodney Scott hit his head with his fist. "And he owes me money!" he exclaimed.

"Owe *you* money!" scoffed Rob, "and how many others! But I'm serving you all notice. No bills going to be paid!"

Nell's eyes widened and flew to Rob's. Was it that bad? It couldn't be – Surely, even if he had to sacrifice the horses for the lowest prices, with two car-loads, there would be enough realized to pay their bills . . .

Her eyes held a definite question. For the first time Rob met her gaze directly and his hard expression gave her a definite answer. Her eyelids fell. It was true. A disaster. But she didn't care. Money – what did it have to do with them?

While the hilarious and senseless talk criss-crossed the table, Nell listened to the music. An orchestra and Arthur Rubinstein were playing a Rachmaninoff concerto. The broad, impassioned crescendos entered into her blood. So men could feel that way too. It had been composed by a man. It was being played by men. It was the way she felt. Was it the way Rob felt too?

At some time during the evening someone announced that it was snowing, and the men went out and closed the windows of their cars. Gus kept bringing in logs for the fireplaces and bowls of *glögg*. It was too late and the weather too bad for anyone to think of driving back to Laramie that night. Nell went into the downstairs bedroom to be sure there was oil in the lamps. Striking a match and shielding the flickering wisp of flame, she suddenly saw another hand resting on the table before her. She could not mistake that hand – the hard power of it – the significance . . .

The flame went out. The hand closed around hers, completely engulfing it. Her hand was lifted and the palm was kissed twice, then dropped.

Trembling all over she found and struck another match. She was alone in the room.

She lit the lamp and stood trying to pull herself together. She looked at the palm of her hand as if she could see upon it the imprint of that violent caress which had been able to turn all the blood in her body into fire.

She would stand there until her trembling stopped and her heart quieted down.

She looked at her hand again and again. She laid it upon her cheek. She wondered if, when she returned to the living-room, the mark of it could be seen reflected in her eyes, on her lips, in her smile, in everything she said, for the kiss continued to burn in her. She could not get it out.

She examined the lamps, made sure there were covers enough on the beds, and stood trying to plan the disposal of her guests for the night. Eight people, five beds, two of them double. She couldn't think. It was worse than trying to place guests for a dinner party.

Her guests planned it for her. Two married pairs could sleep in the two double bedrooms, the two bachelors in the boys' rooms, Rob in the bunkhouse.

16

Nell slept in Rob's dressing-room. If not his own arms around her, then let it be his room.

Not often in a whole lifetime does one lie all night long without sleep even brushing the eyelids, but so it was with Nell that night.

In the morning the men were up early digging out their cars and putting on chains, while the women got breakfast.

They left immediately after, and Rob paused to kiss her and say – this time without even a glance into her eyes, "I've got to go back to Laramie with them – some business to attend to. I'll be home soon. I'll wire you, and you can drive down and get me."

Chapter Thirty-one

Nell dreamed she was being married again to some man she had never seen. He was about six-and-a-half feet tall and broad-shouldered in proportion. He had straight brown hair, getting a little thin, and a very red face of a shade something like the American Indian. He was punctilious, kindly and attentive.

The marriage ceremony took place in the grounds of an estate, shaded by great trees. It came abruptly, before she had attended to certain important business matters. Indeed she had an uneasy feeling that it was not going to be entirely legal until these things were done. Was it the final papers of a divorce? She could not quite be sure – but certainly the way was not clear for the marriage.

The officiating clergyman, too – there was something a little off-colour about him. He had to explain, as he stood before them with a deprecatory smile, that – since he had been told so recently during an adventure (which he recounted to them) that he was now a bona fide priest, he could legally perform marriages.

She and her fiancé were seated before him in two low chairs.

"I know," he said, waving his hands, "that you are anxious and in a hurry –" and she and the huge red man hastily assented and joined their hands as skaters clasp crossed hands in front of them.

The only observers of this marriage were the dozen or two Great Dane dogs who belonged to the estate. She had seen them before in their wire enclosure, hurling themselves against it in an insensate violence. Now, off to one side of the ceremony, they were lying quietly, all in the same position, heads on outstretched paws, the back legs drawn up under. Half of them were dead. These lay in exactly the same position as the living dogs, but they were skeletons only.

Nell felt the feverish dream-misery of having forgotten something important, or lost something, or of being improperly dressed. And while she sat with her fiancé, their hands clasped like skaters, waiting to say *I do*, she felt the eyes of the Great Danes upon her, the living eyes watchful and a little threatening, as if to say, *Be careful now – watch your step*. And the black sockets of the dead ones saying, *It's all no use – it's too late*.

And she awoke with a burst of relief to find it a dream, but haunted by the terrible reality of the big red man with the careful manners, her next husband. He followed her all day, so vivid and unique in appearance, so definite in personality, that when she drove down to Laramie to lunch with Rob and bring him home she found herself nervous, like a woman between two men. And she kept thinking, let sleeping dogs lie. But they weren't just sleeping.

The past week had been almost as hard on Nell – on appetite and nerves and sleep – as the weeks before, and she was thin and strained. But she dressed very carefully in a six-year-old suit of green tweed and a felt beret of the same shade. The fever that was in her lit her face with colour and quickness. Her iris-coloured eyes darted in every direction. Her lips were tremulous. She laughed a great deal. When she took off her jacket and sat there in her thin close-fitting yellow sweater she looked like herself again, bright and young. Rob had very little to say. She had to make conversation and did not know how much she dared ask. "Was it true – about the horses – what you told them at dinner the other night?"

"Yes. I couldn't have chosen a worse time."

"I'm sorry, Rob." She hesitated and dropped her eyes as she said it. "About our debts too? That we can't pay them?"

"We can't pay them."

"And the five-thousand-dollar note?"

"Not that either. That's what I've been doing this week – getting all these things settled. Extensions on the loans and notes, arrangements with our creditors."

This week perhaps, she thought as she cut her lamb chop, but what about last week and the week before? And why couldn't you have been living at home, driving down here in the daytime to attend to banking business as you always have before? But none of this worried her since Rob's visit of a week ago. As long as he loved her – that minute in the dark when he had taken her hand and kissed it! And, too, his absence was explained by the fact

20

that the sale had been a failure and he dreaded to come home and tell her so. *There you are, simply sitting back and waiting for the crash – so that you can pick up the pieces.* She couldn't blame him.

"Tell me about Howard," she said, since he had no intention of talking about the sale. She didn't know yet what the size of the cheque had been. Wasn't he even going to tell her that?

While he talked about Howard and the school, her mind was divided into several parts, listening, pursuing its own course of reflection and analysis, and observing closely.

It wasn't only the hand that had made her sure again of his love. It was having found Gus mending the sleigh in the loft over the stable. And he confessed that Rob had brought it from Denver in the truck and that it was to be a present for her, and that he was to say nothing about it.

Not only the hand and the sleigh, but the Monkey Tree too. Riding one afternoon, she had come upon a big Monkey Tree around which a trench had been dug. She halted Gypsy and sat looking at it with astonishment. This was the way Rob transplanted grown trees. Dig a deep trench enclosing the roots, then soak the earth thoroughly so that it would freeze when freezing weather came. In dead of winter it could be chopped out without disturbing the roots or the earth enclosing them, and dragged to a new site.

So! He had been doing things for her – thinking of her pleasure – all the time he was neglecting her and nearly killing her with unhappiness and anxiety. She almost said, How exactly like you, Rob! But oh, how – *how* could all this misery and unrest be wiped out between them! How could they get really married and at peace together again?

21

While she was observing his appearance and thinking about that she told him of Ken's trip to the Valley of the Eagles.

Dressed in one of the well cared for tweed business suits which he wore so well no matter how old they were, and sitting opposite her at the table in the Mountain Hotel grill, he seemed merely like someone she knew, hardly as much of a husband as the big red man whose image sprang up so readily before her. Waves of almost delirious impatience went through her every few minutes. What a horrible state of affairs – that you did not feel even as intimate and at peace with your husband as you had when you were engaged to him. Married all these years, a sixteen-year-old son, and again filled with the excitement and passion and frustration and fever of the very first days – only much worse.

It was not only his aloof manner, there was a deeper change in Rob. His face was hard, he kept his own counsel, he held her at arm's length – all that she could understand. But something baffled her. There had been some blow upon his spirit and it had struck him down. Some of his vital flame was quenched. That sale! She had to bend her head over her plate to conceal her face as she vividly imagined the agony it must have been to him as one after the other his cherished horses went under the hammer for a fraction of their worth. And they were the accumulation of many years of gruelling work. The ranch was stripped now of all except the young stuff and the band of brood mares.

"Will you be able to buy more brood mares?" she interrupted herself suddenly.

"No."

"A new stallion?"

"No."

Driving home, with the back of the car filled with pro-

22

visions, she would have been happy if only he could have been. But how could a man be happy, she reminded herself, when he had just had the hardest sort of a blow and was more heavily encumbered than ever before? Would she, herself, be happy at this moment, unless, as a result of hours of desperate thinking, she had hit upon a plan which, she thought, would point a way out of their financial difficulties?

How soon should she tell him? Should she tell him now, so that they could discuss it while they were driving home? How should she begin it? *Rob – I've been thinking. And I've got an idea . . .*

She stole a look at his face and decided not to tell it now. He looked so – how exactly did he look? Not bitter today. Nor – nor as angry as he had been before he left, but hard. And very much on guard. That could only be against her. And determined – what was he determined about now? Perhaps just to keep on punishing her. He always said when he got angry he was angry at himself, not her. But even if that was so, it amounted to the same thing. He simply oozed ugliness and it disturbed everyone around him.

"Rob, I've been thinking. And I've got an idea."

Dinner and a highball had mellowed him a little. He put down the periodical he was reading and looked at his pipe and discovered that it had gone out. "What about?" he asked.

"Well – about our finances."

Rob hunted for a match. "What about 'em?"

"Well – I really think that I've thought of something we could do to make the ranch pay."

"When did you think this up?" asked Rob, pausing in the act of lighting his pipe to look at her.

"This week – since – since you were here the other night and said that – that the sale hadn't – paid – the way you

23

expected it to."

"Oh! So you thought you would step in and save the pieces!"

Nell felt consternation. Was it going to seem like that to him? She was silent.

"Well, let's have it," said he with forced joviality. His blue eyes were staring at her over his pipe, and it made her remember Ken's words, "Dad's eyes are the fiercest of all."

"Shoot!" he prodded her.

"Well – it really began with something you said some years ago."

"Ah! Kind of you to remember that! But don't bother to break it tactfully to me, Nell, let's hear what it is."

"You said that the income tax man said that the only ranchers in Wyoming who made money were Dude ranchers. And then you said, *And he knows.*" She glanced up at Rob questioningly, hoping he could not see the fine nervous trembling that shook her body.

"I remember. Go on."

"So that made me think of having dudes."

"*On this ranch?*"

"Yes. We had talked about it a few times already, years ago, you remember?"

"And you always said it would kill it as a home for you, if we did," reminded Rob.

"I know I did." Nell plodded doggedly ahead. "I always hated the idea. But – if we were in trouble – if you needed money – it seemed to me, Rob, I should not let my personal inclinations stand in the way."

She looked hesitatingly at him, and away again. His face was full of anger – rage really – and it was shocking to have to look at him.

"And so," said he in his best sardonic manner, "you simply decided that I was a complete flop. Had failed

24

beyond recovery. And that you had better give up all hope of retaining the thing you love the best – your home. Give that up, make this place – that I have broken my heart trying to make beautiful for you – the camping ground of any Tom, Dick and Harry that wants to squat here –"

Nell looked at him indignantly. "It's not fair of you to put it that way. It would only be a Dude ranch in the summer time. In the winter it would just be our home as it always has been. And what if I did have the notion that I didn't want to have any dudes here? People can change their minds. And if we need the money, and this would make the difference between being able to pay our bills, and not being able to. I would be a wash-out if I could not adjust myself to a different way of living for a few months every summer." Her indignation rose. "It's disgraceful to be in debt all the time. I'd rather do *anything* than that!"

"And you imagine," said Rob in the same sardonic manner, "that you could make the ranch pay with summer dudes?"

"Yes. And that's what the income tax man said, didn't he?"

"People talk about 'taking' dudes. The real word would be 'getting' dudes. Most ranchers in this State would be glad to 'get' dudes if they could. How would you go about getting them?"

"I've already started!" said Nell, on her mettle now. "I've written Aunt Julia, in Boston. She has a huge circle of friends and acquaintances. And two of my school friends, Adelaide Kinney and Evelyn Sharp."

"You expect them to promote your business for you?"

"Not that way! Oh, Rob! You're being simply horrible!" Nell sprang to her feet and stood by the mantel.

"I simply want to get the idea," said Rob icily. "You wanted to tell it to me, didn't you? Go on – tell the rest.

25

I'm particularly anxious to know, now that I realize you have passed on the fact of my failure to your relatives and friends in the east."

Nell was silent for a while, then drew a long breath and said, "They won't have to promote my business. They'll be glad to give me lists of the right people to write to. And they'll let me use their names as reference. And I've made out a letter, setting out the plan, descriptions of this place and everything, and we'd have to have pictures, and all that can be mimeographed and sent to these lists of people. And we have the complete set-up. Practically no investment needed. Some guest cabins, yes – Gus and Tim and you could build them yourselves. And as this is a lovely place, and there's beautiful country to ride in and plenty of horses! And I'm an awfully good cook!"

"God" burst from Rob's lips.

Nell said nothing more. In a moment Rob asked, "You say you've made out the letter?"

"Yes." Nell picked it up from the table and handed it to him. But Rob put out a protesting hand. "No. I don't want to see it, thank you. And I hope you haven't set your heart on this. Have you?"

"Set my heart on it?" said Nell.

"Because I don't like to deny you any of your wishes."

"I know," said Nell hesitatingly. "You're awfully nice about that. I wanted to thank you for – for the sleigh Gus is making – and the Monkey Tree. I do thank you ever so much."

Rob brushed this aside. "It's nothing at all," he said indifferently. "No reason you should not have what you want."

Nell was silent. After a while she said, "Rob, you know this isn't just something I *want* – for the fun of it –"

26

"Isn't it? I thought maybe you were lonesome here with me alone."

"You know it isn't that at all. Rob, you aren't even pretending to tell the truth about anything."

"Just a God-damned liar, am I?"

That struck Nell as funny and helped her recover her poise. "It's because I told you that thing last summer – that the horses would never succeed and it made you mad at me. And you've never got over being mad. And I was thinking afterward that it *was* awful of me, to have knocked everything so – the horses and your work – without having something else to suggest. So I tried to find another plan. That's all."

Rob smoked in silence for a while and Nell sat down again. The fire crackled and a big log fell in two pieces with a shower of sparks.

Rob began to knock the ashes out of his pipe. "I hadn't meant to tell you this, Nell, but I'll have to now. Otherwise you won't be able to understand why I say no to your proposition. I am not going to continue to raise horses as the main production line of the ranch. They can be a side line. I'm going to raise sheep."

"Sheep!" exclaimed Nell. "But that requires an enormous investment! How could we possibly raise the money for that?"

"It's already raised. To begin with, although I did not make the twenty thousand dollars from my polo ponies which I might have made with good luck, I did make nearly ten. That cleans me out of horses. With the exception of the young stuff coming up I'll have nothing more to sell. But I have put every dollar of that, and more too – all I could borrow – into a band of ewes. I investigated the sheep market thoroughly when I was in Laramie. I was lucky in my buy I think. I found these up at the Doughty

27

ranch, near the Red Desert. Fifteen hundred Corriedale ewes."

"When are they coming on the ranch?" asked Nell.

"They're already on," said Rob. "I've got a Mexican as a herder, and we drove them up from Laramie two days ago. We came in the back way."

"But what about Bellamy's sheep? They're out on the back range there. I saw them yesterday."

"If you saw sheep on this ranch yesterday, you saw our own sheep. Bellamy left with his sheep weeks ago.' '

Nell was about to ask "What about the lease you gave Bellamy for another year?" but thought better of it. She did say, "You just said you hadn't intended telling me this yet. Why not?"

"Because it may fail," said Rob coldly. "It's a gamble, like all stock-raising. It looks good now. The markets have been good for several years. With these sheep I ought to net almost ten thousand in one year. That will make a sizeable dent in our debts. And if it continues, in a few years we'll be out from under."

For Nell, the reversal of all she had been thinking and believing and planning was so sudden, she felt flattened out. *Why! then everything's all right! Everything's settled and arranged! Our future provided for – and – and – everything!*

Presently she found breath to say it loud, and Rob acquiesced.

"Yes, everything's arranged."

"And there's nothing to worry about."

"Nothing."

The words faded into the heavy silence. Nell's eyes flickered to Rob. Everything all right – nothing to worry about – and yet, between them, this cold distance and strangeness. What made it? Was it impossible – once the habits of love had been broken – to mend them again?

Even when the cause of the breach had been corrected?

Rob stared at the fire and said slowly, "I would have liked it – this experiment could have been worked out first, so that, when I told you, I could have told you of a *fait accompli* – money in the bank, debts paid, notes met, a going concern – not just, as it is now, one more hope, one more plan, one more good chunk of wishful thinking."

Nell was leaning back in her armchair and made no answer.

"But," continued Rob, "since you have made it so plain that it was not only the horses you doubted, it was me too – and any ability I might have to care for you and provide a home for you –" he left the sentence unfinished.

The clock struck eleven, and Pauly rose from where she had been lying near the fire and staged an elaborate stretch, then ran meowing to Nell.

Nell lifted her automatically.

"That's true, isn't it, Nell?" asked Rob in a sudden direct manner.

"What?"

"That you *have* lost confidence in me?"

Nell did not answer immediately. Finally she said, "Rob – I didn't think you would succeed with the horses. I told you that. But that's not *you* personally –"

"But it was, *me*, personally," he insisted. "You didn't think I was going to pull us through, did you?"

"You never took me into your confidence," said Nel. "You didn't tell me you were going to try a different line. You kept saying it was to be the horses or nothing."

"I suppose that's as good a way of answering as any," said Rob slowly.

A sudden passionate protest flung Nell to her feet. Pauly hit the floor with a little grunt. "I don't see why *confidence* means so much to you! I've never stopped loving you – not the least bit. Suppose some of the confi-

29

dence – was gone? That would be only human – wouldn't really matter between us!"

Rob got to his feet and went about blowing the lamps out, and finally answered, "Just that it – sort of – takes the heart out of a man."

It was still possible, thought Nell, as she walked slowly upstairs. When people loved each other as they had, nothing more would be needed than just one look – one word – her name. *Nell*. There would be no forgiving or explaining, just a sudden coming together and all the discord flung behind them.

But Rob stood in a sort of daze in the centre of the bedroom, as if he did not feel at home there. One hand held his pipe as he puffed it, and he stood watching her as she moved about, turning the bed down, closing the window, taking her nightclothes from the closet and dropping them on the bed.

She went to his chiffonier and took out a set of pyjamas and handed them to him. "Here are some fresh pyjamas for you."

He took them absent-mindedly. Then, as Nell undid the belt of her skirt and stepped out of it, and peeled off her sweater, he said to her hesitatingly, "I'm awfully tired. I think I'll sleep in the other room. Do you mind?"

He looked at his wife.

With just her slip on, she was seated in the low chair, one ankle crossed over the other knee to untie her shoe, her slender and beautiful legs shining in their long silk stockings. Her tawny hair hung loose over the pearl-like skin on her breasts. Her cheeks were exquisitely flushed.

Without raising her head her dark blue eyes slid up underneath her brows and she answered easily, "Not at all. I think it would be a very good idea. I shall probably sleep better myself."

Chapter Thirty-two

People do not die, thought Nell, they are killed by inches, because if you're too unhappy you can't eat, and if you did eat, you couldn't digest, and all through your body the processes are turned backwards.

Sitting at the desk trying to write a letter to Howard – "and we have a lot of snow. It will seem strange not to have you home at Christmas, but you'll get lots of ski-ing there in Massachusetts –"

She raised her eyes to the window and propped her chin on her hand. It was a grey, silent day, with a low sky that seemed full of snow. Yes. Threequarters of life is a slow dying. It's despair that kills us off – slowly or quickly – and I suppose everyone gets a dose of it. Now I know how it works. It works on the glands and they break down, and that ages the body and finally kills it . . .

She dipped her pen in the ink and wrote again, "We're keeping Gypsy in so that when she has her foal we can take care of her. Your father is rabid because she's going to have a winter foal –"

She finished her letter and sealed it, then hurried to the kitchen, looked into the kettles that were simmering on the stove in preparation for dinner and began to set the table.

Sitting opposite each other three times a day at meals had come to be an ordeal for both of them, worse, every week that passed. They braced themselves for it – a sort of horror.

And yet she did not really believe it, and she was waiting, thinking that it would all pass, and that the love, like a stream, had gone underground and was still running there strongly and would some day come up into the sunshine again. Perhaps, she thought, I've had my share of happiness and should not ask for more. But I'm not like that. Nobody is. A little is not enough – always more and more – and we will die if we do not get it . . .

Rob was explaining that he was going off to the timbered hill on number seventeen after dinner to mark certain trees for felling, and she answered, yes, the wood piles needed replenishing.

And to herself she said that she would write an aphorism on the flyleaf of her bedside book that night – "We are insatiable for happiness. To find an abiding beauty – this we seek for all our lives long."

Why didn't he go now that dinner was over? Why did he sit there smoking, looking out of the window? Snow had begun to fall softly.

She went nervously about the kitchen, gathering up the dishes, tidying, running the hot water . . .

This waiting! It was almost as if the air trembled, wait-

32

ing for the word that would shatter the tension. But November passed, and December, and nothing was changed. Rob was dark and hopeless and in a sort of hard frenzy.

I always knew he could do it, whispered Nell to herself. He likes it. Likes his anger and fury. Likes to harden himself. *Confidence!* Silly! They don't understand how women love their children, their men. Confidence has nothing to do with it. Besides, is it true? Is he really hurt or is this revenge?

She could not bear to look at him.

And at last she could not bear to be near him. She planned, all day long, how to avoid him, and drew breath more easily, and could eat, and could straighten up, when she saw his back and his big boots tramping up the hill, disappearing into the woods.

She would run up to the stables and pore over the work-bench where Gus was working on the sleigh. For a time, she could lose herself in a child's peacefulness as she watched him lay the bright blue enamel on the wood, then the red, all the gay Swedish colours. There was to be gold leaf on the swan's head.

As Gus told her this, his kind blue eyes smiled into hers and made her forget everything.

"You luk awful bad, Missus."

She knew that – she hated to see her face in the mirror – especially the eyes, so wild-looking . . .

"You sick, Missus?"

"I don't feel very well, Gus. Nothing special. Just awfully weak."

"Mebbe you go see Dr. Scott."

As Nell walked slowly and unwillingly back to the house, she told herself that it could come to be true that she would want never to see Rob again.

33

Chapter Thirty-three

Nell and Gypsy were both out in the heavy blizzard that hit the ranch near the end of January. Nell because when snow was falling she could not stay in; Gypsy because of that well-known but puzzling natural law which causes animals – if it is any way possible – to give birth to their young in the worst rather than the best of weather.

Nell fought her way across the Stable Pasture hoping to reach a point from which she could see the snow blowing on the crest of the Saddle Back.

Gypsy prepared to drop her foal in the scant shelter of a wooded ridge about a quarter-of-a-mile from the ranch. She had escaped from her warm and comfortable box stall. For years now she had dropped her foals on the wild breasts of the open range and this she was determined to do again.

She had prudence enough to stand in the lee of the ridge, but the blizzard drove through the trees, and drifts began to pile up in long combers. The ground was almost bare between them.

Standing close to a tree in one of these cleared spaces she kept her back to the wind. Her head sank patiently. Her tail streamed between her legs. Her spine humped in cramping pain.

To lie down in the terrible cold was something she didn't want to do. But the pain forced her, and at length she went down in awkward jerks and stretched out on her side. It began again – the gathering of all her strength to a strange, violent straining. She had known it a dozen times before. Through the pain ran hope and love and intense longing. She knew the foal already wanted it. She knew her motherhood.

Except for her age and the storm, the birth would have been routine, for Gypsy had been a successful brood mare and she had never had a sick day in her life. But the years had taken her strength and her teeth were gone and food did not give her much nourishment. The labour was longer than it should have been.

When at length the foal slid out, Gypsy was unable to rise. She made one or two efforts, then her head sank on the ground.

The little one kicked and struggled free of the enclosing sac, snapping the cord that united him to his mother, and suddenly breathed. He should then have been licked and massaged and warmed by his dam but lacking such assistance he managed, after a little while, to sit up. The freezing wind turned the moisture upon him to a film of ice, and his violent shivering made it crackle.

Gypsy struggled to rise and attend to her foal. She

raised her head a few times with weak grunts which caught the foal's ear and drew his attention to her and made him turn his wavering head and his still half-blind eyes in her direction. She wanted him to come closer to her, but she could not hold her head up.

The foal continued to sit there shivering, weaving his head weakly, blinking his ice-edged lids. At last he attempted to get up. Instinct urged him to get to the warmth of his dam's body – the warmth and the milk – and he tried to get his long wobbly legs under him and push himself up. Once up, he went down on his knees, up again, he fell over sideways. Up again, all four legs slid out and he went on his belly. He kept getting up, the blood ran faster in his veins, his eyes cleared a little, he began to move waveringly around the big warm hulk lying on the ground. A strong scent came to his nose and he raised his little muzzle and searched eagerly for the teat where it ought to have been, there above him. There was no teat there.

He dropped his nose disconsolately and stood in a weak shivering curve, his head almost touching the ground. His wet switch of a tail was between his hind legs. He looked like a small naked black greyhound.

He tried again, raising his muzzle and making circles in the air with it. When this got him nothing he began to investigate the prostrate body of his dam. He went slowly and weakly, stretching out his nose. He sniffed, moved on, paused and gave it up. Then he began the tremulous search again.

At last he touched the hot rubbery bag. He knew it instantly and lifted his head into the nursing position. No teat. Only the icy wind and snow. Having lost it, it was some time before he located it again. And again he lifted his head to nurse. Again, no teat.

His head dropped, the bitter disappointment took his

strength away, his knees buckled and suddenly collapsed. But the tide of life was on the flow in him, not the ebb. He got up again, searched for the teat and found it quite soon. He was learning. But what good was it unless it was above him where he could seize hold of it and let the hot drink run down his throat? He had to do something about this! He lifted his tiny soft hoof and struck at his mother, pawing her belly. *Get up! Get up! so that I can drink and live and not die!*

Gypsy was drifting towards oblivion, but that demand drew her painfully back. She raised her head. The foal pawed her again. She knew he could not nurse while she was down. Somewhow she must get on her four weak legs and hold herself up and give him the teat.

In her, life was on the ebb and there was no strength to respond to her will. And yet she did it. She did it the way a thoroughbred will sometimes win a race without sound legs to run on. She forced herself slowly into a sitting position, waited a moment trying to hold up her heavy swinging head, then made the plunge and was up.

Her legs seemed cut off from the heart and brain that commanded them. As they bent and buckled, she leaned against the tree beside her. She thrust out her feet, bracing herself. The foal made a small bleat and took two sprawling steps towards her and again lofted his little muzzle to where the teat ought to be. It was there! In ecstasy he began to nurse.

Gypsy's head dropped. She jerked it up again. Her knees gave a little, she leaned more heavily on the tree, held up against her out-thrust feet.

The driving snow beat upon them both and the pines thrashed and roared.

Up on the mountain a coyote sat on his haunches, pointed his muzzle and gave the long mournful howl that called the pack to him and told them there was going to be good hunting.

Gypsy heard him and knew what it meant for the foal when she had left him. No matter, she could do only this one thing for him – give him the milk which was food and drink, heat, strength, purgative and stimulant all in one.

The foal drank and plucked his head away, making the teat flip and bounce. He seized it again and drank again. He was very much of a prince now, doing as he pleased, commanding this flow of nectar. There was a new miracle of heat and power and arrogance inside him. It was the feeling of bucking. It was beginning now with this first mother-drink. A little more – just a little more food and growth and he would put down his little sea-horse head and kick both heels out to one side!

When his belly was full and tight he stood back. And as if he had told his dam, "That's all – I don't want any more," she released the terrible hold she had over her body and it slowly gave way and slid down.

Nell happened upon the mare and the foal as the whiteness of the storm was changing to darkness.

She fought her way back to the house and told Rob. "The mare's down and the foal is standing there half dead with cold."

They took flashlights and went out. The mare and foal were just as Nell had left them.

Rob fell on his knees beside Gypsy and felt of her. "She's alive anyway." The mare did not move. "Gypsy! Gypsy girl!" There was no response. Rob looked up at Nell and then wildly around. "God! What a place for her to pick! What a night!" He seized the mare again and tried to rouse her. He shouted in her ear. He lifted her head.

"Her eyelids flickered! She's not gone yet! If I could

get her down to the stable she might have a chance!" He thought distractedly of a sledge, a team of horses to drag her . . .

"Shall I go get Gus?" shouted Nell.

"Yes, and could you take the colt? He might follow you. Or you can shove him along."

Alone with his mare, Rob kept at the task of arousing her and bringing her back to consciousness. He got behind her and forced her head up. He tried to roll her body so that her legs would be under her. He kept shouting at her, calling to her, and at that voice — those peremptory commands — she regained her senses. He cheered her on, he shoved against her back until the veins in his neck felt as if they would burst. At last she sat up waveringly.

"Atta girl! Now come on! Gypsy! Up on your pins! Now we go!"

Standing in front of her, holding the halter with both hands, he hauled on it with all his might and lashed her with shouts and curses.

As she struggled he drew her forward and she was pulled up on her feet and he grabbed and held her. That's it! Good girl! Hold on now! You're going to be all right!" She kept her feet, swaying.

Gus and Nell arrived with a bucket of hot mash.

"Ah! That's the stuff. Here you are, Gypsy. Get this into your belly!" He lifted the bucket to her nose. "What's the matter? Don't you want it?" The mare's head swung dizzily. Her eyes closed.

Rob handed the bucket to Gus. "She can't eat. Let's get her home. Come on, Gypsy! Come now, girl! Take a step! That's it! Another now!" As if carried by his voice alone, the mare moved automatically forward. Her head rested heavily on Rob's shoulder. They covered a hundred yards or so. Now they had left the shelter of the ridge and the full force of the storm beat against them. Gypsy staggered helplessly.

"Good God! Why did she have to choose a night like this?"

Her head grew heavier, the pauses between steps longer. With a stream of frantic profanity, Rob tried to hide from himself what this meant. He would have carried her if he could have.

When she went down again it was with a crash that pulled him down too.

The thin ray of Nell's flashlight caught his frenzied face as he disentangled himself and stooped for the mare's head again. "Get behind and boot her, Gus, while I pull on her! She can't stay here!"

Under the pelting ice and wind they spent themselves screaming and shoving and hauling at the mare. She quivered a little. She seemed to hear. She groaned. There were a few spasmodic efforts.

"She wants to but she can't," said Rob, at last.

Kneeling, he drew her head against him so that she could still hear his voice and feel his hands. "Nell, you and Gus go on down to the house. No use your freezing here."

"No use nobody freeze, Boss. You can't help her no more. She don't know nuttin."

"She'd pull through if I could get her to the stables. I'll let her rest a few minutes and then I'll try again. You go see to the colt, Gus. I don't want to lose it. Fix a bottle of milk for it. I don't know whether it nursed or not. Put it in with Flicka. I think she'll be good to it, but watch she doesn't kick it."

Nell went away with Gus.

Rob knelt there in the bedlam of the storm, holding

his mare to life by his voice alone. He did not dare to stop talking to her. Every so often there was a quiver of response – the faint twitch of one ear.

A light appeared again. It was Gus returning. "Dot foal, it got a full belly already. She feed it before she go down."

"Good old girl," muttered Rob, his hands on the mare's head. "You *would* do that. *Thoroughbred.*"

"How did Flicka take to it?"

"Vell – she not make up her mind right away. De colt lie down in de hay. Flicka, she snort und she watch it und she smell it. I tink be all right."

"That's good. But you better watch 'em."

"Sure."

He was alone again.

In sanity of wind and snow. Screaming as of something malevolent on the loose. That desperate loneliness of the soul that comes only a few times in life and seems to form a great cavity into which one slides with increasing velocity. And the dark hulk of his mare lying on the bare ground, her closed eyes and her nose encrusted with ice, her breath coming more and more rarely, more and more shallowly.

"If you could only try once more! Come on, old girl! It isn't far – and we'll have many a good ride together yet!"

The ear twitched a little. He rubbed her throat and head. He knew he lied.

It wasn't only a horse dying. It was the end of half his life and all his young manhood, his young wilfulness. It was the breaking of the last link with the happy beginnings of things. It was the hell of the last few months pulling himself and Gypsy down into it. He crouched lower over her and still that ear moved when he spoke.

41

"Gypsy! . . . Remember all the good times we had . . . the polo games . . . remember, Gypsy . . . remember when we were both young together . . ."

He crouched still lower. Her breathing had stopped. The ear no longer twitched.

For long he sat there, then bent gently over her. He took that ear into his hand and whispered into it, "A good journey!" then straightened up and put his hand over his eyes, pressing them hard.

He heard Nell's voice calling and felt her hands on his cap, drawing the earflaps lower, wrapping a woollen scarf around his neck. He felt the touch of her bare fingers on his cheek and throat.

He lifted his head hastily, scattering drops that were like ice on Nell's hands. "Nell! Where are your gloves?"

"I took them off just for a second."

"Put your gloves on."

Nell fumbled with them. All her body was weak these days. She had hardly the strength to draw on her fur-lined gloves.

"Yes – they're on." She sank to her knees beside him. "Is she –?"

He made no answer. He just kneeled there with the mare's head against him. At last he stripped off his gloves and felt her head, her body, her legs – as if he still could not believe it. The stiffness was beginning.

Nell swayed against him and then straightened up.

"Don't go, Nell!" he cried, loosing one arm and flinging it around her.

"I'm not going," she answered faintly and wondered how, indeed, she would ever be able to make that trip down to the house one more time, or even get to her feet.

"Oh, Nell!"

42

It was a harsh, anguished cry. He flung the other arm around her too and held her clasped tight against him, his face pressed against hers.

Was he crying? Crying for his mare? Nell couldn't tell for the icy snow that beat upon their faces and melted there. How would they ever get home ... how would there ever be an end to this ... Ah, ... there was a change ... he was not just hiding his face in hers for comfort and assuagement of his grief ... his hard cold lips were kissing her frantically ... there was pleading in it ... and shame ... and love ... one of his big bare hands was inside her lumberjack and it felt as if it clasped all of her narrow back and held her naked body against him ... the hand was warm ... how could it be warm ... it was warm ... and something like electricity streamed from it into her ... was it that that made her feel as if she was going to faint ... was it cold and exhaustion ... was it because Rob – because Rob ...

It was ended. The knowledge was absolute and final. And as it turned into pure sensation, searing every cell in her body, the terrible hold she had over herself broke. Rob half carried her as they fought their way down to the house. They passed Gus going up to the mare. He was taking four kerosene flares to put around her body. There was a whole pack of coyotes on Saddle Back now and he had heard them howling.

Nell hurried to the stable in the morning, anxious about the foal. Gypsy's foals were important. Hers had been the two who sold for seven hundred dollars apiece, Romany Chi and Romany Chal. And hers had been Redwing, who sold for two thousand.

She found the foal all alone. He was in the far corner of the stall, his tail-end presented petulantly to her and to all the world, his little sea-horse face turned curiously over his shoulder – not going to miss anything.

Enchanted by the picture he made, Nell burst out laughing, clapped her hands and cried, "Who dat?"

And the foal turned and staggered across the stall to her.

And so was born and named *Who Dat*, out of Sacrifice, by Storm.

Chapter Thirty-four

THE wind had stopped and the hills of the ranch lay in quietness beneath their deep swathings of snow.

There was snow everywhere. The boughs of the trees bent with it. The skies were heavy with it. And it still fell softly and slowly, drifting through the air that rang with the music of distant sleighbells.

On that far mountain a light sleigh zoomed up the white slope behind two black mares that plunged under a long crackling whip.

The mares were wild with excitement. Their heads scattered flecks of foam and at every pause they reared and pranced, shaking the streamers of bells which hung on their harness.

The little sleigh, as gaudy as a child's paint-box, ran

at their heels. The swan was proud with gold leaf and rode with a fixed stare. Every fur that could be found on the ranch had been piled into it, and Nell's face emerged, pink with cold, from a grey mass that had once been Rob's coonskin coat.

"But it's the bells!" she cried. "Oh, Rob! The way they dance and jingle!"

Their talk was not very explicit.

"Patsy! Topsy! You black squaws! Show her what you can do!" He cracked the whip.

The blacks took the rest of the hill at a gallop.

"Like it, Honey?"

"Love it!"

He swung the mares in a right-angle along the slope. Patsy reared and threw a clamour of bells into the air.

"Oh, hear the bells!"

"Wedding bells!"

"Let them out, Rob!"

They galloped the length of the crest of the Saddle Back. Rob's crazy shouts and the occasional pistol-crack of the whip punctuated the peal and shimmer and riot of the sleighbells.

"This is it, Rob."

"This is it, my darling love. Happy?"

"I've never been so happy."

"Forgive me?"

"Oh, Rob –"

"I know you have. But I want you to understand too – though I hardly understand myself."

"I know."

"I've been going through an awful hell. Hating myself. Fighting myself."

"I know."

"Something had to – sort of – *die* in me, before I could give in."

46

"But that's the way it always is. Something dies – so that something better can come to life."

"It was all because I'm so damned bull-headed."

"Well – it seems to me a person has to build themselves around the best that's in them. And let everything else be pared away."

Rob was silent.

"But – the paring away – hurts."

Rob turned the sleigh down the back of the hill and it careened, and Nell screamed and the mares started galloping again.

"Hold on!"

The team whirled through the snow, tossing chunks of it from their hoofs. The motion was so light and swift the sleigh hardly seemed on the ground. It was more like flying. Nell turned her face up and closed her eyes. The falling snowflakes were cool little kisses upon her skin. And they hung on the fur of the robe, big symmetrical stars, perfect little gauntlets, and then melted away.

"Rob, I never thought I'd be married twice."

"*Twice*, Baby! You're going to be married so often you won't know yourself! And always to the same man!"

"Rob, I don't think I'd be willing to change back to my first husband."

"He sure was an egg. Do you mind my kissing you all the time?"

"I'm not at all used to it. I've got out of the habit. I don't know that I can stand it."

"It takes practice. You can sort of work on it."

He took her for a long ride. Off the ranch, down the back road, on plains and past woods that seemed unfamiliar. They swept down near to a wide placid stream that was a dark brown between its snowy banks. The bare boughs of the cottonwood trees that bordered it bent with their weight of snow. A black crow floated

47

through the trees with a wide motionless wing-spread. And then they had flashed past, before the crow had drifted to rest on the white bank. The scene was like an etching, printed on Nell's memory forever.

And lastly Rob whipped the mares up another hill and whirled them around on the crest, and reined them in. They came up on their hind legs and snow flew in every direction.

They were overlooking a little valley in which large patches of grey blotted out the snow. It was the sheep. They stood feeding at long racks packed with hay. From the sheep wagon a little thread of smoke wound upward, telling of the herder's stove and the cosy warmth within.

"There they are," said Rob and there was something sober and humble in his voice.

Nell was silent so long, looking at them, that Rob glanced at her. She met his eyes with a little smiling sigh. "Yes. There they are."

Chapter Thirty-five

Charley Sargent never missed the three weeks' autumn race meet at Saginaw Falls in Idaho, one of the few major or "recognized" tracks in the Rocky Mountain States; and had the same stable for his horses, and hotel accommodation for himself, year after year. Taking his horses down the Continental Divide from a high altitude to one several thousand feet lower gave them an advantage, and he liked the town which lay in the long valley between the Wauchichi and Shinumo ranges and had a season of pleasant autumn weather.

Although the distance from Sargent's ranch to Saginaw Falls was not more than eight hundred miles, he always shipped his horses by rail in charge of his trainer, Perry Gunston, rather than vanning them or taking them in an automobile trailer. This was because the highway made a rather precipitous descent, winding down through several mountain passes; and on the Divide, the unpredictable storms sometimes made the road dangerous or even impassable for trucks. But he himself made the trip by motor.

There were always several events scheduled for two-year-olds, in which Sargent tried out his promising youngsters, and one race, on the last day of the meet, with a ten-thousand-dollar purse, which attracted an impressive entry. It was in this race that Thunderhead was to make his debut, and long before school closed Ken had familiarized himself with the past performances of all winners of this big event. Thunderhead had only to run the two miles on the Saginaw Falls track as fast as he had run it at home to win.

For Ken to hang around his father while the letter containing his report card was being opened, or even to allow the depressing event to catch him in the same room, was so unusual that Rob McLaughlin felt sure something was fishy.

He glanced up at Ken who stood waiting beside his desk with hands driven deep into the pockets of his bluejeans. "Going to take your medicine and get it over with, are you?" he grinned, then looked at the boy's face again. That wasn't Ken's usual report-card face – the face of one waiting for a death sentence. On the contrary, the sensitive face was now flushed with anticipation, gleams of light played in the depths of his blue eyes and one smile after the other rippled across his lips.

"Read it, Dad. Read it quick!" he exclaimed, and watched closely as his father took the card and studied it, item by item.

Rob simply didn't believe it. He shook his head with

bewilderment. "Is this card phoney or what? Do you know what's in it, Ken?"

"What?" demanded Ken confidently.

"Ninety-two in Algebra. Ninety-four in Latin. Ninety-seven in Chemistry, and one hundred in English. What's it mean? Has Gibson gone crazy to give you a card like that?"

"Read the letter," chortled Ken. "He told me he was going to write you a letter – and – congratulate you! "

"Congratulate *me!* " exclaimed Rob. "What in hell about?"

Ken placed his hand theatrically on his chest, bowed, said "Me! " and then threw his head back, burst out laughing, and did a few prancing steps around the room.

Rob read the letter through and abruptly laid it down and turned his head to look out of the window. He was remembering a morning just five years ago when Ken was ten, and a report card had come in which there were asorted marks below twenty, climaxing with a zero in English. And in defence, Ken had made the entirely irre- levant plea – *if you would only give me a colt of my own I might do better.* And he had given Ken the filly, Flicka, and Ken had almost killed himself caring for her. He had also managed to write a composition retrieving his disgrace and causing Mr. Gibson to say that he might have another chance with his class instead of being dropped. Gibson had said in his letter that Ken had a brilliant mind, and Rob had asked his wife, "Did you ever think Ken was brilliant? I've always thought he was dumb."

Rob picked up the card and the letter and read both of them through carefully again. Brilliant all right. How in hell had the kid got a hundred in English? That meant no mistakes at all – or superlative performances every now and then.

Rob pointed at the card. "How'd you get this? Was it

just one composition?"

"You had to be *excellent* all year, and write a perfect composition to end up with."

"What subject did you choose?"

"I wrote about that time I tried to get the eagle feather – you know – down there in the Valley of the Eagles, and the eagle chased me all the way down the cliff and stuck his claws in my belly and it was only my belt that saved me – but of course I fixed it up a little."

"How'd you fix it up? Seems to me that was hot stuff without any fixing."

Ken waved his hands in a suave and explanatory fashion. "Oh, I put in some romantic dope – you know, the sort of things writers write – I had it that I had a picture of my girl in the buckle of my belt, so she – sort of saved my life, you see."

Rob's big white teeth gleamed in his dark face. He looked very pleased. But continuing to study the boy's expression he suddenly had a recurrence of his first conviction. There was something fishy about this.

"Tell me, Ken," he said, "is this absolutely on the level? You really did it? It's bona fide?"

"Sure I did it, Dad," said Ken, his jubilance fading at the realization that a bad reputation is hard to live down. "Don't you believe me?"

Rob thought a moment. "Yes, I believe you. But there's something else. Come on now, out with it! What's behind this?"

Ken's smile vanished and he drew a deep breath, standing there very straight before his father with fists shoved into his pockets. "Well, Dad – I did it – because I wanted – you – to say that I needn't go back to school next September fifteenth."

"WHAT?"

"I mean – not go till a month or two later. You see,

Dad, the ten thousand dollar race at Saginaw Falls in Idaho comes on October twenty-fourth, and that's the race Thunderhead's going to win!" He pulled a folded paper out of his hind pocket. "Mr. Sargent says it's just made to order for Thunderhead. They don't have to be registered horses or to have any past track records."

The racing sheet fell open at the page all of itself and he laid it on his father's desk and pointed to the picture of an elderly man.

"Beaver Greenway!" exclaimed Rob, picking it up. "And his ten thousand dollar free-for-all! Sure – I know about it. I bet that old codger his discovered more dark horses than any other racing man in this country. And bought them, too. It's his hobby. If they win, he buys them you know."

"He won't buy Thunderhead!"

Rob read the paragraph through, then tipped his chair back and ran his hand through his close dark hair. "When did you dope all this out?"

"Last fall, when I went back to school."

"When did you start working for this *phenomenal* report card?"

"Right then. When school started."

"And you kept it up all year?"

Ken nodded.

"Just so you might get permission from me to stay out of school next fall when Thunderhead goes to the post?"

"Yes, sir."

"Put it there, son! I'm proud of you!"

Ken was dazed. His small boneless hand was lost in his father's clasp and shaken hard. He was still trying to explain.

"The thing is, Dad, of course I'll make up all the lessons I lose while I'm out of school. But if I had just

53

asked you, and told you that I'd do that, you wouldn't have believed I could do it."

"And you can say that again, boy! "

"So I had to prove it to you – *before* I asked you."

"You've proved it."

"Dad! Do you mean I can?"

"I mean just that. This brilliant mind of yours seems to work in reverse. Give you horses so that you have no time for lessons and even have to stay out of school and you bust yourself wide open and carry the rag off the bush! "

"Dad – there's something more! "

"Ah! Now it's coming! " Rob's face took on its sardonic expression.

"Two things, Dad."

"Well – shoot! "

"You said last year, when Thunderhead didn't get gelded with the other two-year-olds, that he could go till this year. Does – does he have to be gelded? Wouldn't you just – skip it – Dad? Because he *may* win, you see – and there's a chance that the gelding might hurt him or kill him and anyway if he should be a winner on the race track we'd want to sell his services as a stallion, wouldn't we? And anyway –"

"We won't geld him," said Rob suddenly.

This quick victory was another shock to Ken. Rob raised the report card. "You'll find all your life, son, that *fine performance* will get things for you that nothing else will."

"Besides, Thunderhead hasn't really made any trouble, has he?" It was hard for Ken to get his mind off his horse. "He hasn't tried to fight Banner or get any mares, or – well, not *anything* like that."

"Thunderhead hasn't had a chance to raise hell yet. It's been a godsend that we could leave Touch And Go

54

with him until early this spring when she came in heat for the first time. That kept him happy. Kept him away from the other mares and delayed the beginning of what you might call his sex life. Besides, he's been trained and worked pretty consistently. You can train an animal, you know, for the kind of life he is to live. We've kept him away from the real life of a stallion. But that won't last forever. The time will come. One day his ears will pop, and he'll suddenly thump himself on the chest and exclaim, *I'm a man!*"

Ken laughed. "I hope it won't be on the race track."

"Sex doesn't enter much into the life of racehorses. Stallions and mares race together without any disturbances of that sort."

"I know."

"Well now – what's the other thing? Might as well get it over with."

Ken's face flushed a little. "Remember what you said once, Dad? That I cost you money every time I turn around?"

"I remember!"

"Well – what about the money the race is going to cost? The entrance fee and all that?"

"I see." Rob leaned back quietly and became very thoughtful, rubbing his hand through his hair.

"You're a lot richer now than you used to be, aren't you, Dad?"

"Where'd you get that idea?"

"Well – the sheep –"

"The sheep have got me so deep in debt Thunderhead will have to win races to pull me out!"

"Oh, Dad! Are you kind of counting on him?" Ken's face glowed with pride.

"I'm hoping," said Rob grimly. "I've put a lot of work on that horse myself, remember, and I know he's got it in him. But he's an ugly beggar. This summer will tell the tale."

"Of course you know, Dad," said Ken magnanimously, "anything Thunderhead wins will be yours and Mother's."

"Will it? No. I don't think so. We'd want it to be yours. Then you can pay for all your expenses and your schooling and we'll come out ahead anyway!"

"But *some* of it would have to be yours!"

"All right. We'll incorporate. MacLaughlin and Son. And I'll take what I need for the present and we can get squared later on."

There was a moment's pause. Rob hadn't yet said anything about that entrance fee.

"You're going to have a wonderful big hay crop, aren't you, Dad? Don't you think you may sell your hay – the part you won't need for the sheep or the horses or the cows, quite early – say, in *September?*"

"Got it all figured out, haven't you?"

Ken nodded.

"I don't know when I'll sell my surplus hay. It may pay better to hold it till later in the season when hay gets scarce."

Ken looked crestfallen.

Rob leaned back in his chair. "We'd better count this up now and know what we're up against."

Ken called on his fortitude and stood waiting.

"You're going with Mr. Sargent so the trip won't cost you anything, but you'll be in Saginaw Falls for three weeks –"

"I'll sleep in the stall with Thunderhead," put in Ken quickly. "Lot's of owners do that if they haven't got much dough."

"But I suppose you'll have to eat! Sargent will send the colt with his horses by rail and keep him in his stables in charge of his trainer, so there'll be no shipping or stable expenses. You're in luck there – but Thunderhead's got to eat too. So there'll be his feed bill and the jockey fee –"

"That's ten dollars if he just rides, and twenty-five if he wins," interpolated Ken, "and Dad, please don't say *jockey*. People that *know*, call them *riders*."

Rob ignored this. "And the entrance fee," he finished. "Altogether quite a bit of money."

He looked out the window again, and in spite of fortitude, Ken began to feel wet in his armpits and around his waist.

"But I'll stake you to the entrance fee for the one big race and all the expenses for yourself and Thunderhead."

"You will, Dad? Gee! Oh, Gosh!"

"How'll I be repaid if he doesn't win anything?"

Ken's lips sobered in a line of determination and courage. "I'll work very hard all summer."

"You'll do that anyway," said Rob grimly. "I've never given you the idea you could spend the summer sitting on your fanny, have I? Or just monkeying around your horse either."

"And besides," said Ken, "there's another way I could make money enough to pay you back everything and more too."

"This brilliant mind of yours is getting me dizzy, Ken. How can you make several hundred dollars?"

"Well – you told me once it costs you three hundred dollars to put me through a year of school. See?" He smiled brilliantly at his father.

"I don't see. I haven't got a brilliant mind."

"I – just simply – won't go to school. I could study outside and take the exams – maybe – anyway, I'd learn just as much and my schooling wouldn't cost you anything."

"And I'd spend the money financing you travelling around with your racehorse, I suppose?"

Ken hadn't quite the courage to say yes, but he made a graceful gesture of assent and dashed away.

Chapter Thirty-six

Thunderhead's career was taken seriously by everyone on the ranch that summer, and no one rode him but his trainer, young Ken McLaughlin, who tipped the scale at ninety-six pounds.

During the winter just past when the stallion had been kept in, given a liberal daily ration of oats and hay and exercise and training by Rob McLaughlin, he had achieved a superb development. He was as tall as the Percheron – sixteen hands – and would be even taller when he had his full growth. No longer could it be said of him that he was ungainly or badly proportioned. All his parts had grown together. His legs were long and powerfully muscled, his neck massive and arched, his coat a pure dazzling white and shining with the glossiness of a stallion's skin. Strength, power and wilfulness were still his outstanding characteristics.

He was now shod, and Ken was out with him every day before breakfast, running him on the track. He still fought Ken, he still bucked, but when Ken complained of the horse's dislike of him, his father said, "You've got that wrong, son. If that horse really hated you he'd never let you get near him. He doesn't hate you. He fights you because he likes to. He enjoys it. You're his trainer. You've got to make him do what he doesn't want to do and he's a fighting devil so he fights you back. But I'll bet, when he's waiting up there in the mornings for you to come and give him his work-out, he'd feel pretty bad if you didn't show up."

Touch And Go was still the pace-maker for her big brother, and Rob McLaughlin said, "When I see that filly run, damned if I don't think she's the one that's going to be the racer."

Touch And Go was a regular beauty. Tall and daintily made, with a long reaching neck, straight slim legs, little feet that would fit in a cup, and a playful high spirit that kept her always acting up, always dancing and going sideways. Her ruddy hide was glorious in the sun, and the blonde tail and mane gave her a *de luxe*, made-to-order look.

To Rob McLaughlin her perfect conformation was a justification of his theories of line breeding, and he sometimes studied the racing sheet, making a note of what events were scheduled for two-year-olds. "We might run her too," he said, "put her in the baby class."

The summer passed very slowly for Ken, because it was all a tense waiting for the racing season, and a tense watching of Thunderhead. Besides, it was full of excitement – just one thing after the other. The first excitement

59

was when he got home and found out what was going to happen to his mother. It was hard for Ken to keep his mind from confusion when he thought about that. She had wanted it. Hadn't she said at dinner that night, "I want a Monkey Tree, I want a sleigh all covered with bells, and I want a Little Girl," and of course it was right for his mother to have what she wanted. But it was hard to take. He had argued with her about it.

"But Mother, you've got *us!* Howard and me. Aren't we enough?"

"No. I want a little girl."

"Want her *much*, Mother?"

"Want her lots, dear. Remember how hard you wanted Flicka?"

"It might be a boy," said Ken gloomily, and he added, "Besides, doesn't it hurt awfully?"

Nell was busy putting the laundry away. She counted the piles of sheets she was stacking in the linen closet.

"Doesn't it, Mother?" insisted Ken. "Doc Hicks might have to —"

"Ken! This is going to be a *baby!* And Doc Hicks won't have anything to do with it! "

"Oh, sure — I know that —"

"And as for its hurting — who cares about that?" She had finished stacking and her voice was very gay. "You don't get anything for nothing, dear."

"No." His father had told him plenty about that.

"And didn't you —" her hand was lightly on his head, arranging his soft brown hair so that it did not fall over his forehead, "didn't you sit all night in the cold water holding Flicka — just because you loved her and wanted her so much?"

She was through with the linen and went quickly back to the kitchen. Ken watched her, not answering her out loud but thinking to himself that it was different. How could you love something you hadn't ever seen and be willing, in advance, to suffer for it? With Flicka, he had known and loved her and cared for her for months.

He had to struggle against a feeling of dread when he saw his father watching his mother all the time with such anxiety. It was a wonder he would even let her stack the linen. He wouldn't let her do anything this summer. He himself got up and cooked breakfast every morning, and Tim had to come in and clean the house. Gus churned and attended to butter and cream. Of course, no riding; and there was a new outdoor couch with wheels on the terrace under the pergola where she lay for many hours, not doing anything, her hands clasped behind her neck, her eyes on the sky or the distant hills. Often the hair of her bang was darkened with sweat, and there were tiny beads on her upper lip, and her hands were not steady.

Their father had called both boys to him soon after they got home and had said with his harshest voice and his fiercest eyes, "Don't do anything this summer that will cause your mother trouble or pain or *the least anxiety!*"

"No, sir," he and Howard had answered instantly. Afterwards, they had looked at each other with a long thoughtful look. This was serious. It mustn't be forgotten. Their father sure meant what he said.

Howard's coming home had been another excitement, because Howard was changed. At least he was changed when Ken first saw him getting off the train and riding home in the car telling his mother and father things about the school in a deep voice that never slipped up any more. He was in his grey tweed suit, and the Fedora didn't look funny on his face now.

When he got into a shirt and bluejeans with a bandana hanging out of his hind pocket, Ken began to feel more easy with him. And next day Howard stopped sitting gravely with his mother and father and began to devil Ken

61

and wrestle with him. And on the third day they started to tell each other things. Ken made the acquaintance of Howard's two best friends at school, Jake who was a football star, and Bugs. And in turn he told Howard all about his trip to the Valley of the Eagles, and promised to take Howard there as soon as there was a chance, and undid his belt and pulled up his shirt, and showed him the scar from the eagle's talons. It was still impressive.

Howard was astounded. "And only one leg! I'd like to know how he lost the other one!"

The two boys were in the spring house taking long drinks of milk out of the bucket that stood in the trough of spring water.

Ken dipped himself up a ladleful. "Maybe he got in a fight with another eagle. Or maybe he was born one-legged."

"Aw – don't be a dope."

"Well, calves are born with two heads! Why shouldn't eagles be born with one leg?"

Howard buried his nose in the ladle.

"Howard, those rams were as big as cows!"

"What're you giving me?"

"Well, anyway, as big as two-year-old steers. Honest Howard – no kiddin'. And when they rammed each other they made a big BOOM like dynamite going off. Say! Maybe that's where the word rammed came from!"

"Gee, I'd like to get a mountain sheep," said Howard. "When we go I'll take the Marlin thirty."

"And we mustn't forget our fishing lines – Say! Those trout were whoppers!"

All Ken's ideas were a year larger. The waterfall fell practically from the skies. But he didn't try to describe the Thunderer or the other mountains. They still towered over his spirit and silenced him.

"Gee, I hope everything's there still when I get to see

62

it," gloomed Howard.

They leaned against the waist-high trough, white moustaches ornamenting their upper lips, beginning to slow up on the milk drinking.

"Gosh, it's funny to be home," said Howard. "Home isn't anything like what I remembered."

"How is it funny?" demanded Ken.

"Well – you notice things you never noticed before. For instance, the very minute I got into the house I noticed the legs of the dining-room table; and it gave me a funny feeling. Those legs seemed more like home than anything else. It was just a comfort to look at them."

Ken marvelled about this. "What is it about the legs?" he asked.

"I can't explain, but you'll know after you go far away from home and don't even come back for week-ends or vacations."

Ken registered an intention to examine those legs closely at the first opportunity and see if *he* could get any comfort out of them. Meanwhile he questioned Howard further in the hope that he might have other peculiar ideas.

"And when I'm lying in bed in the morning," said Howard dreamily, "not exactly awake, and not exactly asleep, and I hear a kind of chug – chug – chug – and I wonder whether it's a freight train out on the track or Mother beating the batter for the hot cakes – then I remember back to when I would always be wondering that same thing in the mornings all the years I was a boy – and that makes me feel funny too."

All the years I was a boy. Ken looked at Howard in a startled manner. What was he now then? Surely not a man? Seventeen wasn't a man. But seventeen was not only tall this year, it was straight and had a firm steady walk. *There goes McLaughlin bouncing in line!* Ken looked away. That seemed long ago. Howard no longer bounced. There were times he stood and walked and even drew his brows down and frowned like his father.

All this gave Ken the feeling of the world rushing in on them there at the ranch; and as the barriers of his consciousness were pushed back, he too had a strange gripe in the pit of his stomach and felt that he was growing up.

Then with a wild leap his mind soared away to the thought of Thunderhead and the race, and he had to hang his head and bite his lips. That was the most exciting and biggest thing of all. Not even Howard, with Bugs and Jake and football and a new military walk had anything as big and old as a racing stallion!

Nell lay on the outdoor couch and watched the two boys walking down from the spring house to the cowbarn. They were absorbed in what they were saying to each other. Howard so tall, Ken still a little boy – she was glad of it – there wasn't much time left when they would be boys at all. Howard looked more like his father every day – he drew down his level black brows and the blue of his eyes became more intensely cobalt. And the way his chin jutted. It was going to be a strong face. When he had got a good coat of tan on this summer he would look just like Rob. But Ken looked like *her* – would he ever learn to keep that tousled mop of hair smooth!

She began to gather up loose bits of their boyhood. The way Ken, last spring, on a cold day, had run into the kitchen and lifted one of the lids off the stove and stuck his nose down to the hot coals to get it warm!

The way he still ran upstairs on all fours.

The way he was still sure – as he always had been – that she could look at him and "read his heart." "Look at me, Mother, can you read my heart now? What does it say?"

64

The hay ripened early that summer and because there was going to be a heavy crop, Rob McLaughlin got a big hay crew and a cook to cook for them.

He had blasted the rocks out of the two largest meadows early in the spring, before the grass started growing, and then had filled in the holes and seeded them, and even this first year, there would be new grass there, and by next year it would be as thick and strong as anywhere on the meadow.

He wasn't able to do any blasting in the meadows during the summer time, because the tramping and hauling would ruin the grass. But he was going ahead with his plan to develop several little draws.

He explained it to the boys. "The hay is a *sure* crop. You can always be disappointed when you try to sell your horses, or beef, or sheep, for that matter. But hay can always be sold, so it's of the utmost importance."

Now that there were not so many horses, Rob had more time for other work, and the boys too.

Rob gave them one draw which they were to convert into meadow-land all by themselves. A dam had been thrown across the upper end of it and irrigation ditches dug down the two sides on a level with the dam gates. Now the draw had to be grubbed out, bushes hauled up by the root, rocks blasted and the pieces taken away. They had the use of the big team, Old Tommy, the broncobuster, and Big Joe, the Percheron, and a rock sledge, and all summer long they toiled at it.

At noon, Rob would drive the car into the meadow where the hay crew was working and give them their dinner there. Howard and Ken, up in their draw overlooking them, would see the car and drop their tools, hastily put the nose-bags of oats on the horses, then run down into the meadow to get their share of the hot corn beef and cabbage and potatoes and bread and butter and pie and milk.

After dinner they had an hour's rest – Ken was sup-
posed to make up the sleep he lost early in the morning
riding Thunderhead – but this was the time they talked.

"Gee, Howard," said Ken. "I wish you could stay to
see the race."

Howard lay on his back, one knee up and the other foot
resting on it.

"Well, I can't," he said calmly. And it made Ken remember what his father had said. "If there's something
Howard wants and can't have, he's philosophical about
it."

Howard flexed his arm and said contemplatively, "Gee!
This rock-lifting gives a fellow a wonderful development.
I might let Jake and Bugs come out here next summer."

"Would they come?" asked Ken with awe.

"Sure. They'd be nuts if they didn't. This sort of work
really sets a fellow up. Besides, everybody in the east
wants to come out west."

"You know, Howard! Gee! Sometimes I just can't believe it."

"Can't believe what?"

"That it's all turning out to be *real* about Thunderhead."

"Real? Why you dope – what fun would it be if it
wasn't real?"

"Well I dunno –"

"Were you just pretending about it all?"

"Oh, of course not!" Ken was puzzled about that.
How can you be planning a thing in a real way thinking
about it nearly all the time, and yet it is more of a dream
than a reality, so that when it suddenly comes true and
has to be geared in with actual events, hours and dates
and weighing scales, and entrance fees and shipping

66

arrangements, it is just as much of a shock as if you had never really expected it to happen.

Howard was squinting one eye, and then the other, making a hawk that was floating high up move from one end of a cloud to the other.

"When we get to Saginaw Falls and change these heavy shoe's he's wearing to light aluminium shoes they'll feel so light on his feet he'll go like the wind."

Howard held a finger in the air above his face and looked at one side of it and then the other.

"And if Charley Sargent buys Dad's surplus hay and sends it down to Saginaw Falls for the race, then Thunderhead won't have to change to a different kind of hay from what he's used to. Besides, Charley can sell it down there for fifty dollars a ton. He said so. Mountain hay is the best, and down there they'll pay anything if they think it will give their nags a better chance. *But nobody can beat Thunderhead!*" Ken went off suddenly into one of his wild bursts of joy, rolling over backwards and trying to stand on his head.

"Can't you do that?" said Howard contemptuously. He got up slowly, stood on his head with ease and nonchalance, then lay down and stretched out again.

"Gee, Howard! Do you know something?"

"What?"

"I think so much about Thunderhead that when I see my own face in the mirror I'm surprised."

"Hah! You goof. Do you expect to look like him?"

Ken giggled. "Sure, I see him in my head all the time – that long fierce face and his nostrils going in and out snorting, and the red lining to them, and those white-ringed eyes rolling at you, and when I pass the mirror, if I saw his face in it, I don't think I'd even notice it, but when I see my own face I'm surprised and for a second I wonder who it is!"

Howard sniffed at such childishness. "Say! When shall we go down there – to the Valley of the Eagles?"

"Let's go soon. Golly, I hope that one-legged eagle is there! I'd like to pay him back for what he did to me."

"Maybe we could go this week-end."

"We won't say a thing about where we're going," said Howard. "It might worry Mother."

"No. Just off for a camping trip."

"Yes. But I bet Dad won't give us any time off till we've finished this draw." Howard looked at his watch. "Hour's up. We'd better hop to it."

They removed the nose-bags from Big Joe and Tommy, hitched them up to the sledge, and left them by the fence. The two horses had got used to the blasts of dynamite and watched the proceedings with interest.

Ken held the rock drill and Howard swung the sledge-hammer until a deep enough hole had been drilled in the rock. Then they stuck the fuse into the stick of dynamite, tamped it into the hole with mud; then lit the end of the fuse and retreated to the far edge of the draw beside the horses and waited to hear the explosion and see the pieces of rock fly. Then they put on their heavy leather gloves, drove the team down into the centre of the draw, loaded the broken rock onto the sledge and hauled it away.

By night the boys were so groggy with sleep they staggered to bed at eight o'clock.

But it was not until that draw was finished and another one as well, and all the hay put up, that Rob McLaughlin said the boys could have the rest of the summer to do as they pleased in.

Rest? There wasn't any rest. September was here, and there were only four days before the date for which Howard's return accommodations had been taken.

But four days was twice as much as they would need. So they announced that they were off for a camping trip,

68

and Nell put up provisions for them, and Thunderhead and Flicka were hung with bags, rifles, slickers, frying pans, and the boys rode away up the Saddle Back.

Under their feet the bare rolling hills and soft burned grass – beyond, the Buckhorn Mountains, a wilderness of forests and peaks. And an infinite distance away and above, as if borne up on the lower crests, a gleaming shape misted in clouds – the Thunderer – beckoning to them!

And how eagerly they answered. Not the antelope nor the jack-rabbits fled more swiftly over the plains than the four young things, wild with excitement and freedom, galloping south with yells and shouts and pounding hoofs, and their faces cold in a wind that was sharp and sweet with snow.

Chapter Thirty-seven

From the moment of leaving the ranch Thunderhead was in a state of intense excitement. And when they had climbed the Saddle Back and headed south, his wild eyes and his nostrils and his pricked ears never ceased exploring those mountains ahead of them. *His* mountains! *His* valley! – from which high fences and stern masters had kept him for a year.

He was hard to hold when the smell of the river reached them. Ken let him go and he galloped on the little trail he had made himself until they rounded the hill and the Silver Plume river came into view. While the horses watered, the boys debated whether they should stop and fish, or try to complete the trip that night; and because of Howard's limited time decided on the latter.

Thunderhead took the lead and they plunged into the mountains. He was filled with a fiery and masterful energy. He had never forgotten; and now that the way was open to his inherited destiny, he was ready and eager for it. His stallion's consciousness had come of age at last.

It was already twilight in the gorge; and under some of the overhanging cliffs and great trees the trail led into darkness. But Thunderhead went swiftly; and when the boys stopped to pause and look and exclaim at the plunge of the great waterfalls or the foaming cauldrons of white-water, his iron shoe struck the rock impatiently, and his strident neigh tore the thunderous roar of the river.

The scent was getting stronger, and it maddened him with joy. It was the scent of destiny, of a life, of an overwhelming emotion. For not under the saddle or running obediently around a track, but here in these mountains lay his whole existence and he had carried the flame of it on his conscience for a year.

That evening they pitched camp in the park-like grounds not far from the base of the valley rampart.

Picketed with Flicka below the camp Thunderhead did not lie down and sleep as a young horse should. Only older horses, who no longer have growing pains, sleep standing on their feet. But Thunderhead stood all night long, his body quivering, turned to that rampart and the pass into the valley, his ears pricked to catch the faintest sound.

He knew it immediately when, in the early dawn, a group of mares and colts drifted through the pass to gaze in the park here below the rampart. He nickered and started to run to them, but was pulled up by his picket rope and stood there pawing impatiently, nickering again and again.

Flicka woke up and was also seized by the excitement of meeting strangers. Thunderhead ran around the circle allowed him by his picket rope. He backed away, lowered his head and gave it a few shakes, pulling at the rope. But his training had been thorough. It was now almost a physical impossibility for him to fight a head rope. He plunged a bit, and then reared up, pawing the air. When he came down he whirled and looked at those mares again – just dark shadows in the vague grey dawn – then he dropped his muzzle to earth, placed one forefoot on the rope, with a little fling of his head got it between his teeth and bit it through as neatly as he had bitten off the leg of the eagle.

With an eager neigh he trotted off towards the mares, leaving Flicka impatient and unhappy, nickering lonesomely, but too docile to attempt escape.

Ken had been dreaming all night of the playful nickering of horses. He dreamed he was riding Thunderhead on the range in a band of yearlings, but why did they keep nickering so? What was attracting their attention. There came an uneasiness into the dream. The nickering persisted but, as if attempting to present a plausible explanation, the dream changed rapidly. Now he was riding Flicka in the brood mare bunch. And now he was riding the corrals on the day of the weaning, for that was surely the nickering of young colts . . .

Ken's dreams became still more uneasy, and he sat up suddenly and saw the dawn and knew where he was and could not understand why the nickering continued even now that the dream was ended.

There was one dazed minute in which he sat there, collecting his wits, brushing the sleep and the hair out of his eyes, and then he realized that off near the rampart was a group of mares and colts with a white horse among them, and that the nickering came from them.

It was just what he had seen on his former visit to the valley except that this was only a small number of mares; and the Albino, for some reason or other, was not behaving like a sensible stallion but was rearing, squealing, whirling around to face first this one then the other, in fact was a living coil of movement and excitement.

But there was nickering closer at hand too, and suddenly Ken became anxious lest Thunderhead and Flicka should be excited by the proximity of the strange mares and break away from their picket lines. He flung back his blankets, leaped out of them and ran down stream. It brought him up sharp to see only one horse there. Flicka hardly paid any attention to his arrival. Her ears were pricked toward those strange mares, and she pawed the ground, and it was her nickering that had aroused him.

In a daze, Ken picked up the second picket rope and looked at the end of it. Bitten clean through. He dropped it and rubbed his hand through his hair. That was Thunderhead over there with the mares then, not the Albino! No wonder he had behaved peculiarly. Thunderhead with mares at last!

Ken's mind began to labour. He must be got away from them immediately! The Albino might come out through the pass, looking for those mares. And suddenly near-panic seized Ken. The race so near! And the least injury to Thunderhead at this date might make it impossible for him to run.

Now he thought fast. He picked up a nose-bag half-full of oats and walked very quietly over towards the mares.

As he drew near, he called Thunderhead softly and held out the nose-bag and shook it. The oats made a rustling sound. That was enough, as a rule, to draw twenty horses at a run. But Thunderhead merely turned his head to glance at him, then gave his attention to the mares again. Now and then he would drop his nose to the ground and half-circle the mares – plunging at them – turning, dodging, snaking them. It looked as if he were going to round them up! Ken became more alarmed. If he rounded them up, he'd get them going and he'd go along with them, and it would be still harder to catch him!

"Here boy! Here Thunderhead! Come along, boy. Here's your oats – oats, Thunderhead! OATS!"

Thunderhead paid no attention. With more determination now, he drove at the mares. He whipped around them, got them moving, drove them towards the cleft in the rampart.

Ken stood still, appalled by the realization that the horse had actually taken possession of the mares. They gave him complete obedience, as if the electric power within him had welded them all into a unit of which he was head and master.

Suddenly Ken ran forward again. "Oh, Thunderhead! Come, boy! Oats! Come get your breakfast!"

"Hey, Ken! Ken!" rang out behind him. "What's up?"

As Howard came running, Ken looked at him speechlessly. Howard saw Thunderhead driving the mares through the gap, and he too halted.

"Holy Smoke!" he exclaimed.

Thunderhead and the mares disappeared in the twistings of the passage. Ken began to trot after them and Howard followed. Ken was still calling desperately, "Come, boy! Get your oats! Here Thunderhead! Oats!"

The passage narrowed. They were going through the keyhole, passing directly underneath the great boulder which hung over it, and the next moment there was the wide spread of the valley before them, ghostly with a faint luminescence through which the dark forms of the horses moved like shadows.

Then light flooded the heavens and shafts of rosy gold poured up from the rising sun to bathe the snow-covered peaks of the Never-summer Range.

Not even the disaster of Thunderhead's rebellion could lessen the impact of this sight upon Howard.

"Holy Smoke!" he exclaimed again and stood motionless.

But Ken's agonized eyes found what they were looking for. The Albino, and his instant alert as Thunderhead entered the valley! The two stallions saw each other at the same moment. The Albino rushed forward as if for immediate attack, then turned and began to round up the far-flung band of mares and colts behind him. At a swift twisting gallop he circled them, gathered them all in and bunched them in an invisible corral. All his actions were strained and nervous.

Thunderhead moved with exuberance and calm. His muscles flowed smoothly under his satin coat as he leisurely circled his little band of stolen mares, bunched and froze them, then trotted out in front.

The two stallions faced each other about a hundred yards apart, motionless as statues. The Albino moved forward a little, then stopped. He did this again. Thunderhead stood without a quiver, his head high, his weight forward, his hind legs stretched back.

Ken suddenly thrust the nose-bag into Howard's hands. "Hold that! They're gonna fight! I've got to get him!"

He ran to Thunderhead, calling his name. Thunderhead did not even twitch an ear in his direction. He was watching the Albino with a minute, comprehensive stare that penetrated the body and timed the nerve-fuses.

Ken seized the dangling haltar rope and flung his weight on it. "Come away! Come away, Thunderhead!"

He hauled with all his power, trying to break the stallion's fixation, but he might as well have tried to move a rock. The stallion stared over him, immobile.

The boy burst out crying and struck at the stallion's head, jerking to and fro with all his weight. "Oh, stop it,

Thunderhead! Please, Thunderhead! Come away!"

Howard dropped the nose-bag, rushed to his brother's side and seized the halter.

Ken's voice reached Thunderhead dimly but he made no response. This was his world, his inheritance, Ken had no part in it. But how to become master of it! Only by the destruction of that which barred his way.

Rearing backward, he shook loose, knocking Howard down and snapping Ken aside with a whip-lash of his head. Then, screaming his challenge, he hurtled forward as from a spring-board.

At the same instant the Albino rushed to meet him and both animals stopped short about thirty feet apart and stood tensely eyeing each other. These were two antagonists who had met before and had not forgotten the event.

Mingled with Thunderhead's desire to annihilate this obstacle before him was the satisfaction of an intense curiosity. Here at last was the great being who had overshadowed his whole life, the image of whom had hung in his blood as persistently and as challengingly as the snow-scent hung in the mountain wind.

But the Albino was confused. His feet shifted nervously as if taking firmer hold of the earth. His reaching nostrils expanded and contracted slowly. In his sunken eye-sockets his white-ringed eyes stared and meditated, seeing there before him, HIMSELF! His own superb and invincible youth! He was there! He was here! But the strength was as one. It flowed like a current between them as if it were already creating a third horse that appeared in a misty globe between them, and in which they were both fused.

Power and fire and glory rushed through the old stallion and he trumpeted with ecstasy at this transmutation of himself into the shining magnificence of that vision.

He rushed forward. One will seemed to animate them both, for Thunderhead charged too, each flinging bared teeth at the other's back in passing.

The Albino drew first blood. A red stain sprang out on Thunderhead's withers and spread slowly down his shoulder.

As they passed, they whirled and reared to strike at each other with their front hoofs, reaching over the neck to land body blows that resounded like great bass drums. Short snarling grunts were jarred from them.

The Albino reached under and seized Thunderhead's throat, trying to pull back and tear out the jugular vein. But Thunderhead locked his forelegs around the Albino's neck and pressed close into those grinding jaws.

The horses staggered like wrestlers, Thunderhead forcing the Albino backwards. Then he loosed the grip of his forelegs and began to use them for attack, flailing with his hoofs on the back of the Albino, raking the flesh from the bones and striving to land a crippling blow on the kidneys.

For an instant the massive jaws crunching down on Thunderhead's jugular vein relaxed, he tore loose, both horses wheeled, plunged away, then whirled to eye each other again and to get their wind and their balance for the next charge.

There was a jagged bleeding gash in Thunderhead's throat. The Albino was laced with pulsing crimson streams. The unnatural expansion of his nostrils showed the beginning of exhaustion.

Again, as if animated by a single will, the stallions charged each other with high heads and stiff, lifted tails. Meeting, rising, swerving, sinking with indescribable coiling grace – not one motion lost – they turned their heads sideways with bared reaching teeth and thrust them forward and under to seize the foreleg.

Each blocked this manoeuvre cleverly; they braced themselves against each other with locked, straining necks, and swung back first one and then the other foreleg out of reach of the darting, snake-like heads. But Thunderhead was as quick as a rattler. His muzzle thrust in and caught the lower leg of the Albino before he could withdraw it and fractured the bone with a single twisting crunch of the jaws.

The Albino gave no sign. The moment Thunderhead loosed his hold, the older horse rose to his full height. One foreleg dangled useless, but he still had that mighty right hoof with which he had nearly killed the colt two years ago. The same blow would do it now.

Thunderhead too was on his hind legs, feinting as if to strike. But he saw the blow coming. In mid-air he whirled, dropping his head and lashed out with his heels.

As the Albino came down with his killing stroke, his face received the full impact of those terrible hoofs, and both cheeks were ripped up so that the skeleton of his head was bared.

The Albino's one good foreleg hit the earth with a crashing jar. Thrown off balance by failure to land his blow, and the murderous kick, he sank to his knees. Before he could recover, Thunderhead had spun around. His right hoof shot out in one pawing stroke which crushed the bony structure of the old stallion's head and sliced off the lower part of his face.

Blood spouted from the fatal wound, mingled with the choking and bubbling breath. The Albino's eyes closed and his body sank into the earth, his head moving slowly from side to side in agony.

Thunderhead stood over him. The Albino's eyes opened once and looked up at Thunderhead! There was the vision. The shining phantom horse – oversoul of the line! To this prince of the royal blood he now bequeathed all his wisdom. He gave him knowledge of the voices of the trees and waters and the great snows and winds, so that nothing

78

in the valley would be strange to him, no, not a single mare, nor the smallest colt nor a humming-bird nor eagle nor a blade of grass.

Thunderhead's right hoof rose and fell with lightning speed, cleaving the skull.

The Albino quivered and was still. Then one deep sigh came from him, and on it there ebbed away his life, while his blood and brains pumped slowly out to mingle with the earth of his beloved valley.

Thunderhead lifted his mighty crest and made the mountains ring with his unearthly screech of triumph.

Chapter Thirty-eight

"Stand Thunderhead!"

Hardly had the echoes of Thunderhead's cry of victory ceased than a small familiar figure was beside him, commanding him.

Obediently Thunderhead stood while two hands seized the halter rope and gripped his mane. Ken vaulted onto his back.

The stallion's eyes were on the mares. All through the fight they had stood in two close bunches, watching, fascinated. Now that it was ended they began to disperse. They were confused and nervous.

Howard picked up the nose-bag of oats and started towards Thunderhead. But the stallion suddenly plunged towards the mares. Ken flung his weight back, hauling on the rope, but it was whipped out of his hands as the great white head jerked impatiently, then dropped, snaking along the ground. The stallion was not only beginning the round-up of the mares, he was taking command and making himself known to them as their new master. Ken seized handfuls of the thick, wild mane.

Thunderhead galloped faster. He swept in a huge circle, whipping the two groups of mares into one. Then, as if merely to discipline them, he bored through them, scattering them again. They dispersed over half-a-mile. And now he began to herd them at full gallop. Not for a moment was he straight between Ken's knees. His body was in continual undulation. Ken was riding the end of a whip-lash, twisted mercilessly. Occasional cries of pain and help-lessness burst from him. The stallion was driving the mares and colts further up the valley and they were all running now, increasing speed at the furious coercion of their new master.

A black runaway mare with a little white colt at her side streaked out at an angle from the band of mares, bent on escape. Thunderhead altered his direction and took after her. Ken felt the great body underneath him knotted and gathered for a sudden turn or stop – for any one of half-a-dozen manoeuvres; and, unable to ride with his usual free, balanced seat, clung like a monkey.

The stallion came abreast of the mare and closed in. She did not surrender.

Ken knew what was coming and flung himself back, braced for the shock. The stallion reached over the mare and seized her neck in his powerful jaws, jerking it towards him, and at the same time threw himself back on his haunches.

Ken was flung sprawling on the horse's neck.

The mare's body went over in a complete somersault and she crashed to the earth, rolling over and over.

Ken, clinging to Thunderhead's neck, was, by a miracle, still on.

The mare got shakily to her feet. Thunderhead galloped after the herd and now she followed him obediently.

He reached and passed the mares, and took the lead. The black mare forged to the front of the band and the little white colt galloped mightily as if trying to reach the side of the stallion.

Wave after wave of nausea went over Ken. His face was deathly white. His body ached as if it had been beaten. His fingers in Thunderhead's mane clung merely because they were stiffly locked. He had lost all hope of ever getting control of his horse – the hills were sweeping past – he could not stick on any longer – the herd was thundering behind him. Where was Howard? Where was the keyhole, and safety, and Flicka? At this pace, he was leaving them far behind.

There came at last a moment of anguished exhaustion when he cared about nothing – only to be off . . .

He loosed his grip, flung himself flat back on Thunderhead's broad rump, at the same time swinging one leg over his withers. From this side-saddle position he slid to earth. His feet touched for a second, then he was hurled on his face.

He felt the jarring thud of the ground and lay there. The thunder of the herd roared up and over him. The ground shook. Clods of dirt and stinging gravel pelted him and abrupt blocks of light and darkness alternated over him as the big bodies of the mares lifted in the air to clear him – one after the other.

It receded into the distance – that thunder of hoofs – until at last it was not even so loud as the sound of the wind in the pines, and his own heart-broken sobbing, and the harsh far-away cry of eagles who dropped from the clouds to feast upon royal carrion.

Chapter Thirty-nine

The command not to cause Nell any anxiety had been disobeyed. For the boys, riding double on Flicka, hardly got home in time to hurry Howard into his clothes and pack his suitcases.

After he had gone, Ken sat down by his father's desk in the study and told the details of all that had happened.

Rob was in a very quiet mood. He sat in his square wooden chair, turned slightly towards Ken and puffed at his pipe.

"Why in God's name!" said he at last, "did you take Thunderhead to a place where there were mares and another stallion?"

"But Dad!" exclaimed Ken woefully, "he'd been there often before! And he had his own regular place to watch them from – perfectly safe – up there on top of that rampart! He never went into the valley, not since that first time when he got the awful swat when he was a baby!"

"And so you figured he'd continue to do as he always had done. And that's where you made your mistake. After all, Thunderhead's three years older now, and in some ways, for a horse, that's grown up."

Ken's tired and dirty face turned away and his eyes wandered, then came back to his father. "But he's never done any hell-raising. And he's been trained for running and racing. You said yourself a horse will develop the way he's trained."

Rob's slight sardonic smile showed a line of white teeth beside his pipe-stem. "There's still nature, my boy – don't forget that –! God made horses, you know, Ken. Not domestic horses, to labour and toil for men. Not racehorses – *prima donnas* in stable-boudoirs, with valets and ladies' maids and trainers – but *wild horses!* Stallions and mares, with intelligence to take care of themselves. He made the stallions to breed and take care of the mares, fight for them, round them up, make them obey, see that they have proper food and shelter. He made the mares to have their foals and take care of them. They drop them out on the hills. The cord tears loose, drains blood for a little while – that is as Nature intends. Then it dries up and falls off and there's never an infection. Nature takes care of it – not a veterinarian. It's all very well to call it hell-raising when Thunderhead begins to live and behave as we don't want him to – but that's Nature. And if you forget that, you've got a jolt coming."

Ken sighed deeply and wearily, nodding his head. Well, he knew about Nature now.

"And between you and me, Ken," continued his father, "every horse-lover in the world has to take off his hat to *the wild horse* – a horse that acts like a horse – as God

84

made him – not according to some cooked-up plans of men."

Ken gave perfunctory attention to what his father was saying but his mind was on one thing only. Where exactly was Thunderhead now? How exactly could he be got back?

"We hunted up there at the far end of the valley as long as we could," he said. "If Howard hadn't had to get home, we would have had more time. I wanted Howard to take Flicka and leave me up there for a while. But he wouldn't. He said we had to stick together."

"Quite right. It would have been dangerous. Besides, you had no horse. How would you have got home?"

Ken averted his eyes, ashamed to say that his father or Gus would have had to come for him. "I might have got hold of Thunderhead again."

"Ah! A pretty long chance!"

There was a silence while Rob sat in thought. Then he said, "Have you any idea where he took the mares?"

"Well, we went far enough up the valley to see that it went out into other valleys, and then other valleys branched off of those. There wasn't any real rampart – that volcanic wall I told you about – up at the other end – just a lot of mountains going up one behind the other, higher and higher. That left a lot of places where the horses could have gone. It just looked like a – a – labyrinth of mountains and draws and gorges and valleys –" Ken turned his head away again, oppressed by the memory of the scene – the clouds of snow, the blazing glaciers, pockets of emerald grass, the soaring grandeur of the peaks. He couldn't even try to put it into words.

"It was just hopeless. There wasn't a sign of the mares or Thunderhead. We had trailed them all the way up the valley – of course it was easy to see their tracks, especially Thunderhead's. But for the last two hours it snowed. I think it snows every day up there. And it was getting dark."

"What time was it when Howard found you after you fell off Thunderhead?"

Ken thought a moment. He wasn't going to tell his father that he had lain there sobbing his heart out for an hour. "Well – I don't know exactly – I was asleep –"

"After you fell off?" Rob glinted a little looking at his son.

Ken flushed. "Yes. I was so dead tired. And – and – I just lay there. When I felt Howard shaking me and looked up and saw him and Flicka there, I didn't know where I was or what had happened for a moment. But I think it was about noon."

Knocked cold and didn't know it, thought Rob. Aloud he said meditatively, "You sure can get yourself in the damnedest predicaments! You must have as many lives as a cat! Anyone else would be dead if they'd been caught in half the jams you've been in! First with Flicka. And then the eagle got your gizzard. And now this."

Ken's head swayed in complete agreement.

Rob smoked for a few moments. In his mind the scene lived again.

The hidden valley, the fight of the two stallions . . .

"God! I'd like to have seen that fight!" he exclaimed.

Ken wagged his head wearily. "You just oughta have seen it. It was like – it was like – Dad, you know those prehistoric monsters?"

"Dinosaurs and pterodactyls and mastodons?"

"Yeah. Those. Well it made you think of them. They both looked so big – as big as elephants – maybe that was because they were up on their hind legs all the time and their heads so high and their hoofs pawing. And then after Thunderhead had won, the way he stood up and screeched! Dad, if there were any monster roosters in prehistoric days, and they *crowed* – that's just the way

Thunderhead was. You could have heard it on the tops of those mountains. It went right through you like something filing on glass – only as loud as a locomotive."

"And that's when you walked up to him and mounted him?"

Ken nodded with another of the deep sighs that expressed his physical exhaustion.

The mere thought of it made Rob get to his feet and walk round the room. "It's the God-damnest thing that ever was! Why, Ken! didn't it occur to you that all he had to do was throw out one paw the way he did to the Albino and it would have gone through your head like butter!"

"But he wasn't mad at me. He didn't pay any attention to me at all."

Rob dropped in his chair again. He was bursting with pride. He leaned forward and squeezed Ken's knee and in spite of himself the boy winced.

"I suppose you know that it doesn't often happen that a man rides a stallion in the act of rounding up a band of mares and lives to tell the tale."

Ken nodded his head in bewilderment. "He was awful queer. He didn't mind having me around or on his back, but just didn't seem to notice me, or hear anything I said. And he wouldn't obey me at all any more." This last was in an aggrieved tone.

Rob shouted with laughter. "Obey you! I should say-ay-ay not! Who are you to interfere in a moment like that?"

Ken tilted his head assentingly. The joke was on him all right.

He had a look Rob had seen on him many times before – always caused by one of these soul-struggles over horses. He was white and hollow-eyed and looked as if he'd lost ten pounds.

"You look like a picked chicken," said Rob dryly. "You

always manage to get yourself all run down just when it's time to go to school."

"School!"

"Yes. But I suppose we ought to be thankful that you came home all in one piece."

Something was choking in Ken's throat. School again! Just school! After all the year's hopes and the work and the planning! After having been a racing man! Owner of the wonder horse! Practically over with such childish things as school! And already possessed of his father's permission to stay out of school and go to Saginaw Falls with Charley Sargent!

Rob's eyes were running over him critically. "You look pretty sick. Aside from dirt and scratches and getting tuckered out, nothing happened to you this time, did it? No claws in your belly? No broken bones?"

Ken raised his right arm carefully and moved it about in an experimental manner.

"What happened to that arm?"

"When I slid off Thunderhead and saw I was going to land on my face I threw this arm up – gave it a crack."

Rob examined the arm and shoulder. Ken winced several times. "Nothing broken. Anything else?"

"Well, coming home on Flicka – I couldn't straddle her, my legs ached so – I had to sit side-saddle."

Rob laughed. "I've had that feeling myself. That came from riding the stallion when he was snaking. It wrenched every muscle in your body."

Rob's eyes went over Ken minutely, noting the rugged, filthy clothes, the hands with dirt ground into the hasily washed scratches and abrasions, a dark bruise down one side of his face, stains of blood inside one leg of his blue-jeans.

"I did think I was a goner once," said Ken.

"When was that?"

"When I fell off Thunderhead and the mares were coming right behind."

"No horse will step on a living thing if it can be avoided. And I suppose they were pretty well scattered."

"Well – they weren't spread much –"

"If they have time to see, they'll jump."

"That's what they did. It was as if the light went on and off. It would be light over me, and then dark, and I'd get a squint of hoofs and belly – then light again. But they sure spattered me all over with dirt and gravel."

"I'll say they did. What's that blood on the inside of your pants' leg?"

"That's from Thunderhead," said Ken.

"Was he much cut up?"

"A lot of bites and rips. A deep one on his side and shoulder that I got all this blood from. It was the very first wound of the battle. Then he got that bad one in his throat I told you about, but nothing seemed to bother him. He didn't act as if he knew he was wounded."

"Probably didn't. And probably the Albino didn't know he was killed. I often think pain and death don't enter into the consciousness of horses at all. What about your friend, the one-legged eagle? No sign of him on this trip?"

"He came down. Six of them came down to eat up the Albino."

"Ah! They'll pick his bones! A true burial of the plains!" Rob's face lit up. "A great old boy! I've always had a corner in my heart for him, even if he did nearly brain me!"

Ken had forgotten this. His father showed him again the scar over his temple where the Albino's hoof had left its mark and it seemed to draw them all into a close little knot.

"What a great horse!" said Rob leaning back again.

"Ken, there are outstanding individuals in the animal world as well as the human. The Albino was like Napoleon! Or like Caesar! To be close to one of those is like being close to a charge of T.N.T."

"Yes, sir," said Ken wearily.

He knew.

Rob made a little gesture with his hand. "Well! The king is dead! Long live the king! "

"You mean Thunderhead?"

"Thunderhead. The Throwback." And that took them both back to the day three years ago when the ungainly little white foal had been born and everyone had thrown at him the epithet, *Throwback!*

"Dad –"

"Well?"

Ken hardly dared to say it. "Do you suppose if you took a lot of men – maybe ten or twenty – with horses and lariats up the valley – I could show you the way – you could get him back? Because you see there's only a little more than a month before the race –"

Rob answered gravely, "It would take a regiment of cavalry – and *then* they wouldn't get him."

Ken was silent. He was not surprised. Moreover, deep within him, something revolted against the idea of taking such an expedition into his valley. The band of mares broken up, some of them killed during the roping, colts stolen, separated from their dams, coarse shouts and curses and brutal acts desecrating that remote, inviolate animal sanctuary – he'd almost rather lose his horse.

Ken lifted his white face with a look of straight-seeing courage and resignation in his eyes. "Dad," he said again, and paused. For the hundredth time in his tortured mental processes he had come to the same conclusion – that there was only one slim hope. "Won't he come back, Dad?"

"Of his own accord?"

"He always has before. This is his home and he's oriented. You always said he would, and he always did."

There was a little sadness in Rob's sardonic smile this time. "Ken! You know horses! He's got a band of mares now, hasn't he?"

"Yes, sir."

"Will he abandon them?"

The question needed no answer. Ken had reached that same conclusion in his own thoughts every time.

His head sank on his chest and Rob saw that the boy was trembling all over. He hadn't yet had a bath or change or a night's sleep or a solid meal.

"You go clean up now, son, and get ready for supper, or you'll be keeling over. You've had a great adventure. It didn't end the way you wanted it to, and I'm as disappointed as you are about losing Thunderhead."

"Oh, are you, Dad?" Ken raised his head and his eyes went to his father's face. Somehow it eased the pain to have his father disappointed too.

"Yes, I am. I've worked with him. And I had come to have confidence in him and his future. He's a great horse. Besides, you know, I needed the money—"

"I know!" Ken's face was almost happy.

"But we're both out of luck and we'll just have to take it."

"With fortitude," suggested Ken with a gleam in his eye.

"Exactly. No use crying over spilt milk. I can tell you this, if it'll make you feel any better—" They both got to their feet. "I'm damned proud of you!"

"Of me?"

"Of *you*. My God, Ken! *You rode a stallion at work!* No one but a fool even goes near a stallion when he's rounding up his mares — let alone tries to mount him — or could stick if he did!"

91

"I didn't stick."

"Sure you did – till he darned near killed you. You behaved with courage. You tried to get your colt back. You tried to master him. You got on him and rode him to hell and gone. You did something I've never done – and I'm proud as punch!"

Ken was overwhelmed. "Of course," added Rob, "I suppose all this was to be expected from a fellow who once pulled off such a stunt as to get a *zero* in English! I never did that either!"

Rob dropped a hand on his shoulder and shook it. "Now go on and get a good hot bath. Put all this out of your mind. Supper'll be ready in an hour and I want to see you eat! And I've got a surprise for you – something you'll like. I'm going to talk it over with your mother first."

Ken lay in his hot bath, luxuriating. All the sore knotted muscles eased and relaxed, and the feverish pain was drawn out of the scratches and abrasions.

He began to feel much happier. His mind was packed with vivid memories as glorious as thunder and lightning and rushing winds, and his own forever.

He measured out some of his mother's bath salts. He had heard salts helped take the ache out of your bones – it said just a tablespoon, but when you were so lame probably you needed a bigger dose – he emptied half the bottle of perfumed lilac salts into the tub, then lay back and stirred it up with his toes.

He examined and counted all his wounds, while his mind rolled forward on a fascinating scale. Thunderhead would always live in that valley with his mares, but he would yearn and grieve for Ken, and Ken would visit him now and then, and Thunderhead would be glad to see him, would even let him ride him – (though not while rounding up his mares).

He noticed that his head rested easily on the back of the

tub while his toes were braced against the end. Surely that was new. He used to float uncomfortably. Ah! Maybe it was beginning now! The shooting up process!

All the while he heard the murmur of his parents' voices in their near-by bedroom and that made him happier still, for his father said he was going to talk it over with his mother and it was something nice.

Drying himself gingerly standing on the bath-mat, Ken decided that he most certainly was taller.

He got the iodine bottle from the medicine chest and attended painstakingly to his wounds. He was dotted and smeared all over when he finally sat down with slicked hair and startlingly clean fingernails to the supper of fried chicken and mashed potatoes whipped with hot cream such as only his mother could make.

And again he told and re-told the story of his adventure, even to the bit about the black mare who made the dash for freedom. "She was a beauty, Dad. She reminded me of Gypsy, only she was bigger. And the white colt — he was like Thunderhead used to be. He had short legs. He scrabbled."

And at last Rob told his boy of the important thing. That none of his plans need be changed. He could still go to Saginaw Falls with Charley Sargent. He could still send a racehorse of his own in Charley Sargent's express car. There would still be a Goose Bar entry in the races. The only change would be that it would be the two-year-old filly, Touch And Go, instead of the three-year-old stallion, Thunderhead.

And so when the big black Buick rolled down the mountain passes of the Wyoming-Idaho highway on October eleventh there were two racehorse-owners sitting in the front seat, Charley Sargent, quite formal-looking in a black overcoat and Derby hat, and Ken, feeling at least ten years older than ever before.

Chapter Forty

Ken's sudden ageing was because of several things. The trousers of the new suit he wore were two inches longer than any he had had before. And a small Fedora hat sat upon his knees, carefully guarded against possible wear and tear.

But the greatest change was within him. It was so peculiar a feeling that he looked inside himself to inspect and name it. He decided finally that it must be fortitude. He had made acquaintance with the real article at last, and he knew it as an admixture of bitter disappointment with cheerfulness and readiness to go on and do whatever was in line. He wasn't "howling" about Thunderhead now when the worst had happened.

Several new experiences were grouped around the new state. When you were howling you could derive pleasure from nothing except the one thing you wanted which was denied you. But when you had fortitude, a great deal of pleasure could be built on top of that, even though, at the bottom, was still the deep grief. For instance, he was enjoying this ride immensely.

Riding in an automobile, people feel as if they are very busy doing something important; and that, therefore, nothing else can be demanded of them either by their own consciences or by external busybodies. This is a great comfort to nervous people, and since everybody is nervous, to everybody. When one is enjoying this freedom from duty and coercion one even resents being asked to turn the head to look at the outline of those hills back there. Or to move a little to see if you're not sitting on my glove. No nuance of this subtle pleasure was wasted on Ken. He felt very conscience-clear, very grown-up, and very lazy.

Ken was also enjoying Charley Sargent's company. The tall horseman seemed different somehow in these clothes. The Derby hat took away some of the geniality of his humorous face and gave it a shrewd wariness instead. But when he glanced down at Ken there was much friendliness in his eyes.

"How long d'you reckon it was you sat on that stallion, Ken?"

"Oh, I dunno – long enough!"

"I'll bet! My God! Say – how many mares d'you think he had in the band?"

"I never had a chance to count 'em, but there were a lot, spread all around."

"Maybe thirty?"

"Maybe."

"Tell me about that fight, Ken, just how they went at each other."

"But I told you all that, Mr. Sargent."

"Well, I want to hear it again." And when Ken had complied, "God! What a horse!" he nudged Ken with his elbow. "And don't you forget, Appalachian was his sire!"

He would have gone on talking and hearing about the Valley of the Eagles and all that had happened there indefinitely, but Ken wanted to get information about the race-track they were going to and the business of racing horses in general.

"Well, Ken – this track at Saginaw Falls is as sporty a little track as you could find anywhere. You know there are a few tracks in this country that are just run by a bunch of millionaires who like to take money away from each other. This is one of them."

"How do they take money away from each other? Betting?"

"Yes – and sellin' nags. Now listen, Ken – you're not to do any bettin', get that in your head."

"I've got five dollars," said Ken.

"Well, hang on to it. There are two ways to make money with racehorses – or to lose it. One is bettin', and one is raisin' horses and sellin' 'em. The last is my line, although I place some bets too. But *you* can't be a racin' man, Ken – travellin' around the country, runnin' horses and bettin' on 'em –"

"I know I can't."

"And even if you could, I wouldn't want it for you, and neither would your Dad and your Mother – no matter how much money you made."

"I know."

"What you are is a breeder and trainer of horses. You've done a grand job with this filly, she's right on edge

96

for a winnin' race, and she hasn't been coddled, she can run any distance – in her class, that is. And on any kind of track."

Ken felt a glow inside and looked up with a slight flush.

"I may bet on her myself," added Sargent, "She's a speeder and no foolin'. She might go right to the front and never be headed. She'll run in the event for maidens on the sixteenth – that's five days from now. She's already sharp as a tack so we won't have to give her any fast work which might reveal her speed. Nobody knows her, and odds'll be long against her. I may make our hotel bill on her." He glanced down at the boy, grinning.

"It sounds cock-eyed," said Ken.

"Racin' *is* cock-eyed," said Sargent, "except in the bull-rings where it's just a bunch of horses runnin' against each other and the beetle that runs the fastest gets a purse."

Ken thought that sort of race would be much more sensible. "Couldn't I sleep with my beetle in her stall instead of in the hotel?" he asked.

"You're goin' to sleep where I do. And that's not in the stables, young man."

Ken sat silently going over in his mind all that would presently happen to Touch And Go. She had been shipped from Sherman Hill four days ago with Sargent's four horses. She was at Saginaw Falls now in charge of Sargent's trainer, Perry Gunston, being exercised by Tommy Pratt, Sargent's exercise boy. And on October sixteenth she would run her maiden race. The Condition Book listed other races for two-year-olds on October twentieth and another on the last day of the meet following the Greenway race. With three chances, Touch And Go ought to show – if she had it in her.

"What rider do you think you'll get for Touch And Go, Mr. Sargent?"

"I'll get Dickson for her if I can. He's ridden winnin' races for me before and he's a good kid. But if I can't get him, there are a couple others just about as good – Green – Marble –"

Ken immediately made pictures in his mind of Dickson, Green and Marble. He liked Dickson the best. He could see him, in Sargent's colours, mounted on Touch And Go – out in front, drawing away to win! And at this point Ken's heart always skipped a beat or two.

They were dropping rapidly down from the top of the Divide. The weather had been stormy and the rolling hills spreading out on either side were blown with snow that here and there let the brown earth through.

Charley Sargent drove at about eighty or eighty-five miles an hour, as most men do in the west where great distances have to be covered and there is little traffic on the roads.

They stopped every few hours at wayside stations, and Ken would sit beside Charley Sargent at the counter and would have to go through an agony before he would know what to order, while Charley, in the twinkling of an eye, would have ordered a cup of coffee and a piece of pie.

They ran in and out of snowstorms. You could see them ahead! far away. The air would get thicker and darker, and suddenly you would be right in that storm, you had caught up with it, presently you ran out of it again.

Everywhere were mountains. They sprang up unexpectedly not half-a-mile away at a sudden turn of the road, or there was a fall of miles and miles, a wide valley lying purple-dark at the bottom, and far distant ranges of mountains shining white in the sun, turning to misty blue when clouds covered the sky, vanishing altogether in mid-afternoon, and blazing out in the sunset against a sky like the inside of a furnace.

Sometimes the wind would burrow into the snow and sweep up a bunch of it into a little cyclone, and Ken would watch it spinning along the plains, turning into the shape of a waterspout, and it would remind him of the plume of snow the wind lifted from the Thunderer when he was in the mountains. And the memory of that brought a sudden emptiness inside him that made him gasp.

Thunderhead! Where was Thunderhead now? No . . . think of Touch And Go . . . think of the little filly, so bright and gentle and docile . . . so beautiful with her dancing step and smart style . . . think of her airy lightness, her extraordinary speed . . . think back to the day you first saw Flicka run . . . run away from Banner who was chasing her on the Saddle Back and she was only a yearling with a pink-blonde tail and mane, and she showed Banner a clean pair of heels . . .

Touch And Go was just Flicka all over again. Ken loved her with the gentle protective love that a mother gives to her second-born when the idolized first-born has died.

His thoughts sprang to his mother. He had been wishing for a long time that a person could have fortitude for someone else. He would like to have it for his mother and give it to her, but it wasn't possible. Fortunately, she had it for herself. He had discovered that, one evening standing in the empty dining-room with the door open into the kitchen. His mother was getting supper in the kitchen, and suddenly he heard a sound from her. There was no one in the kitchen, but she was talking out loud as if there were, and he heard the words, "Oh, will I ever be young – and slim – and quick – again!" and then a soft little moan. And he had turned quickly and looked through the door and she was leaning against the wall with her back to him, her head tilted over, one hand hanging straight down at her side with the dish towel in it. And it made him feel so bad he hurried out of the dining-room and outdoors and wandered around in terrible confusion of mind until supper time. He felt he ought to tell his father, they ought to get the doctor, something ought to be done right away. But when he went in to supper, there was his mother just like she always was, with quick smiles for all of them, and that serene look about her dark blue eyes, and a face flushed pink from the stove, and a ready laugh if there was anything funny. That was her fortitude.

Well – it wouldn't last much longer! And then she *would* be quick and slim and young again. He wished he knew just when it was going to happen. Several times he had been on the point of asking the exact breeding date but had refrained for fear it might not be considered polite.

No matter how fast Charley drove, the world was so vast it didn't sweep past them, it stayed there. There were white-faced Hereford steers and cows grazing on the barren-looking ground. Horses too – all of them with thick warm coats for winter. And now and then a close band of grey sheep, hardly visible in the grey air. They made Ken think of their own sheep. Perhaps his father was out looking them over at this very minute, talking to the Mexican herder, planning just when they would put the bucks into the band with the ewes, planning for spring lambing.

Sometimes Ken napped. When he spoke again it was the same panorama of hills and plains and distant ranges, part snow, part rock, part bare brown earth, and the same Herefords and horses grazing in the foreground.

During the two-day trip to Saginaw Falls there were three passes to descend. They reached the first in a snow-storm and were blocked by a truck coming in the opposite direction which had ascended the grade and slid sideways on the very summit, nearly closing the road. Behind the truck were several dozen east-bound cars trying to get up the grade.

As Sargent stopped his car and waited for the truck to get out of the way, other cars came up behind them and waited too, skidding on the snow-coated road as they put on their brakes. Sargent and Ken got out and walked forward and looked down the grade. For a mile, you could see the east-bound cars that had been held up by the jam on the summit. They were in every sort of crazy position on the road, tilted on the inner bank, or two or three of them locked together with their occupants stamping around in the snow, shouting at each other, pulling or shoving at the machines. Men in shirt-sleeves, and bare-headed to save their hats from blowing away, squatted on the ground, trying to untangle their chains and put them on.

To get past the truck every west-bound car had to crawl out to the very edge of the road where it overhung the abyss, squeeze around the truck – and this could not be done too slowly because the wheels would lose traction – and then wind and slide in and out among all the stalled cars on the down-grade.

Charley knew the road well and had taken the precaution of having his chains put on at the last service station. But there was no chatting as he negotiated the pass. Ken looked at his face but did not speak to him. Now and then the boy cast a fascinated glance over the edge of the cliff to the right – that sheer drop into a dark chaos – it seemed a mile!

At the bottom of the pass they got out and Ken helped remove the chains.

"It's bad enough without snow," said Sargent as they put the chains in the back compartment and got into the car again, "those hairpin turns – now you see why I send the horses by rail instead of bringing them in vans or trailers down this highway."

101

"I should think," said Ken, as they hit the straight-away and Sargent increased his speed, "that cars would go over the edge of that road sometimes."

"If you look at the daily papers," said Charley, "you'll find that that's a very frequent occurrence."

Ken could see it in imagination. The big black thing rolling over and over – bouncing – falling through sheer space – perhaps one or two tiny human forms dropping out of it and going down like dolls, head over heels – then the crash at the bottom. It made him feel sick.

"Or," said Charley, "while you're driving these roads you'll often see a break in the little fence at the edge – if there happens to be one – where someone's car has gone through. Or you'll see a tree broken. Of course, the passes aren't always as bad as this one today. The first real snow catches everybody unprepared. By tomorrow the snow-ploughs will have just about cleared it. They have to, otherwise the trans-continental buses couldn't keep goin'. Even in the worst storms, they keep the roads open. If they can't clear them, at least they break up the surface so that cars with chains don't have much trouble."

Ken hugged to himself the picture of Touch And Go as he had last seen her, cosy and safe in the express car with Sargent's horses, and bales of hay and sacks of oats for the journey.

"Mr. Sargent, if Touch And Go does turn out to be a winner, wouldn't you like to take her around with you to all the meets you go to and run her on shares with me?"

"Ken, I've got too many of my own already. I'm al-ways tryin' to sell, not to buy, nor to add to my over-head. Perry can take care of only so many horses, you know, without hirin' more men. Your best bet is to sell her if you can."

Ken wondered if anyone would want to buy his filly. When it came right down to it, it didn't seem possible.

that someone would buy Touch And Go and give him a big cheque that he could take home to his father.

There were other passes, but they were running out of the snow-storms as they reached the lower altitudes, and the last pass was a really thrilling sight – as if a giant mountain of granite had been split by lightning and the two sides leaned apart, and the road and foaming white river wound down between them in a lost world of stone.

Ken peered from the window. It was like the Silver Plume River. It *was* the Silver Plume – swiftly leading him away from the highway and the race track and taking him back to the gorge and the valley and the mountains and Thunderhead . . .

"Better close that window, Ken –" Charley reached a hand over and wound up the glass.

Ken leaned back, suddenly sick with longing for his horse.

It was getting late. Sargent put on the lights and the car hurtled westward through the darkness.

Chapter Forty-one

Thunderhead lifted his nose high and searched the wind.

It was a bare craggy peak overlooking the southern end of the valley that he had chosen for his look-out. From here he could see below him where his mares were grazing. He could turn and look at the tiers of mountains behind away up to the Thunderer in his eyrie in the sky. He could see the clouds rolling around them, he could hear the deep rumble of the giants that lived underneath, the fall of every avalanche, the crack of every frozen tree; and not a bird nor animal could move without his eyes and ears taking note of it.

It was an uneven pinnacle of rock on which he stood, with barely room for foothold. His hind legs were braced down and apart. His body was twisted. His head, with its floating white mane and spear-pointed ears, was lifted high, his dark, white-ringed eyes filled with the wildness of the mountains and the clouds. Dangling from his black halter was a bit of rope, frayed and worn at the end.

A little below him, baulked by the steepness of the last sheer ascent, a small white colt stood looking up at him. Now and then Thunderhead's glance rested on him for a second, then brushed past and up again.

A new message was on the wind this early morning. There was a heavy storm coming. The temperature was twenty below already and still falling.

The mares and colts were protected by a long thick growth of hair which they had started growing in September in preparation for this early storm. But Thunderhead was warmed only by the inner heat of the stallion. His coat was, as always, silky and shining, scarred only by patches of rough, long hair under his throat, and on his shoulders where he had been wounded.

Around the mountain peaks many storms were tossing, rolling down the slopes, colliding with each other, carried on opposing currents of air. A boiling mass of wind-cloud swept north over the valley with an eagle sailing before it. Now and then the storms united and came down in a deep white blanket, then were broken up again and, roaring, separated and moved in every direction. Gradually the smother thickened and snow fell, driving first one away, then the other.

Thunderhead reared his crest high into the storm. His mane streamed to the west. The eastern wind was strongest and would prevail. *An easterner*.

Memory tingled through him and his pawing hoof rang on the rock.

When the cold burns too deep, when there is death in the wind, take the way down the mountain. Gates are open. Mangers are full of hay. There is shelter and food

105

and kindness for all. And the screaming whiteness cannot follow you in.

He made several abrupt movements of his head, then turned and picked his way down the crag, his tail sweeping over the white colt, who carefully followed him.

Thunderhead rounded up his mares and headed them north down the valley. When he had them running he took the lead, with the black mare and her white colt close behind him. His pace was carefully chosen so that the smallest colt could keep up.

What snow there was boiled like sea-foam around their feet and there was that sound in the steadying eastern wind – that unvarying roar – that would turn into a whine as the velocity increased.

They strung out single file going through the keyhole and down the river gorge. Now and then Thunderhead circled to see that there were no stragglers, giving a few nips to keep the tail-enders aware that they were on a drive and expected to keep up.

Below, on the plains, they spread out, kicking and biting, wild with the heat of their blood, and the excitement of the run, and the fierce beating of the wind and snow.

They neared the ranch in the late afternoon, Thunderhead swinging along at a canter, finding his way through the white smother with the ease of an infallible instinct. He was on his own ground now, and had known every square foot of it since birth.

Reaching the crest of the Saddle Back, he halted to survey his domain and his mares crowded up around him. Nothing could be seen through the snow, but to his inner eye, every building, every fence post was visible, and as he plunged down the slope he indulged in some coltish bucks of pure joy. With those thirty handsome mares and colts behind him he could be forgiven for feeling the pride of a young heir when he brings home his bride and displays her to the family.

Down the Saddle Back they poured at a full gallop, up the County Road – the gate was open! Thunderhead made the sharp turn, the mares following close, cantered down through the Stable Pasture to the corral – again the gates were open! They poured in . . .

It was already full of mares and colts. All the familiar old smells! Every brood mare as comfortable to him as mother's milk! Oats and hay. The corral and stables. Banner . . .

Thunderhead nickered and squealed in an ecstasy of homecoming. He plunged through the mares to the feed racks and tore out a great mouthful of hay – Castle Rock Meadow hay that he had been brought up on. His mares pushed in behind him, mixing with the other mares, starting little fights and scuffles.

Banner met him in the centre of the corral. The two stallions stood nose to nose, quivering and squealing, half rearing. They were filled with the excitement that goes with the meeting of old friends – and something else, too, because of those mares and colts. They turned away from each other and began to investigate. Thunderhead's approach to the Goose Bar mares was the greeting of old friends, but it was different with Banner. These strange mares were new and exciting! There were so many of them – and his own quota was incomplete. With a mere ten brood mares any self-respecting stallion is looking for more.

The mares and colts milled around, crowding the walls of the stable and the feed racks.

Banner pursued three of Thunderhead's mares that were in a little group together. His head snaked along the ground. He drove them over to a group of his own. Thunderhead tossed his head high over the crush where he was feeding at the rack and his flaring eyes caught sight

107

of this manoeuvre. He dropped his muzzle to feed again. Banner continued to move Thunderhead's mares from where they were feeding over into a corner of the corral and to freeze them there.

Thunderhead wormed himself out of the jam. He pursued Banner and neighed challengingly. As the red stallion turned and faced him, they both reared and nipped, then dropped to earth and stood quivering.

In Thunderhead was all the old love for Banner, but there was another feeling too, and it was getting stronger every instant. Anger. Combativeness. A furious uprising and outpouring of energy that lifted and stiffened his tail and burst from him in squealing grunts of protest and sent him rearing and pawing into the air. It would presently find an outlet in more dangerous action then that.

The two stallions plunged past each other again and this time each aimed an ugly nip in passing.

"Boss! Boss! T'underhead is here mid a big bunch of mares und colts!"

Thunderhead knew that voice. It went with the oats and the shelter and the kindness.

"Coom qvick, Boss! Dere all mixed up wid our mares – de stallions is fightin' –"

He knew the other voice too that answered from the Gorge, the deep, commanding voice with the anger in it. And he knew the two faces as they appeared through the driving flakes – the round pink face with the grey curls framing it – and the long dark face with the white teeth showing in a wind-beaten snarl – he knew the smell of them, but not this other smell of consternation – this smell of shocked horror. Nor the panic of that voice when it shouted, "Get the ships, Gus! Bring a couple of pitchforks!" Didn't know the arms that flailed him and beat him back with frenzied shouts, "Turn Banner's mares into the other corral – he'll follow them!" Even while he plunged past the man and reared again and Banner reared to face him and each aimed a smashing blow over the other's neck that landed like a dull thunder-clap, he had to take care to avoid this man who lashed his head and face with a whip, who hung, yelling, on his halter, who interfered in every possible way with his fixation, who flung his whole weight and heft against him, turning him, while the other man turned Banner . . .

There was confusion flooding his brain . . . snow-wind blinding his eyes . . . obedience conflicting with libido . . .

The barn. His own stall and a manger full of hay and oats. How had this happened? How had he got shut in here? He loved this stall. He dipped his head in the manger. Lifting it, he listened and pricked his ears and reached his sensitive nostrils into the air and fluttered them. . . . He could smell each one of his mares and colts. They were all there, around the stable, feeding at the racks . . . everything all right . . . all safe and cared for while the blizzard whined and the wind seized the barn and rattled it like a dried pod . . .

"Can you beat it? Thunderhead came back in the storm and brought his new harem! Habit was too strong for him."

Rob made a practice these days of hiding his temper from Nell, announcing even serious news in a careless manner.

So for a moment Nell was deceived and turned from the table where she was placing the silver for supper and looked at him with wonderment and joy.

"Thunderhead back again! Oh, Rob!"

Rob stamped across the kitchen floor to wash his hands at the sink, and it seemed to Nell that the grin he flung over his shoulder at her was more of a toothy snarl than a smile.

"Where is he now?" she asked.

"I've got him shut into the stable."

"I'd like to see him. I'll go after supper."

"You will not!"

As he turned towards her, snatching the towel from the rack and drying his hands violently, she saw the wildness in his eyes. She said nothing more but set the supper on the table, and as Rob went to his place, he leaned over and kissed her and said contritely, "I can't let my darling be doing such reckless things as that at this late stage of the game."

Why is that reckless, thought Nell, then suddenly asked, "Where's Banner?"

The frenzied look Rob flung at her opened up to her understanding the whole scope of this predicament.

"I've got him in the east corral with his mares – and Thunderhead locked into the stable."

"Is he – is he safe there?"

"Not any too safe. You know that old stable. Horses have got out of it. Flicka beat her way through one of the windows. Thunderhead broke through the top half of the door once – hope he doesn't remember it –" Rob was wolfing his supper. "The two bands of mares and colts are all mixed up in both corrals – eating me out of house and home – eighty head of horses! Gus and I'll have to spend half the night sorting them out – putting them through the chute – Banner took some of Thunderhead's mares and put them with his –"

A look of consternation dawned on Nell's face. "He did! Why, Rob! Why, that might start a fight!"

"It might and it did!" Rob reached for bread.

"Oh, Rob! What did you do?"

"We beat them apart. Just in time, too – before they

110

really went berserker. A little later and we couldn't have done it. One of them would be dead now."

Nell was stunned into silence. Rob ate hungrily, then added more quietly, "And it wouldn't be Thunderhead."

Nell said nothing to that. No. Certainly not the powerful young creature who had overcome such an antagonist as the Albino – no – it would have been Banner . . .

"Rob," she said quietly a little later, "do you think they're safe now?"

"I do not." Rob shoved back his chair, went over to the stove and stood with his back to it while he filled and lit his pipe.

He took a few puffs, drew the smoke into his lungs, felt the calming effect of it, and finally took his pipe out of his mouth and held it, his eyes fixed in a brown study on the floor and said, "Banner will never be safe again."

"But – but –" stammered Nell, "we can send Thunderhead away again – he'll go back to that valley with his mares –"

"And in every storm he'll bring them home," said Rob quietly. "He's done that all his life, he'll continue to do it."

And for a while there was nothing to be heard in the cosy kitchen but the whine of the wind around the chimneys, and a sudden furious onslaught rattling the windows.

Pauly crawled out from under the stove, stretched slowly and sensuously, curling up her coral tongue, then seated herself and began a leisurely and thorough bath.

"No," said Rob again with a sharp sigh, raising his eyes to the ceiling of the room and taking a few more puffs of his pipe, "Banner will never be safe – not till Thunderhead is dead – or gelded."

A sound burst from Nell. "But Rob – *Ken!* And at that Rob went wild again.

"I'm thinking of Ken too!" he shouted. "Do you think I like to do this? Now, when the boy has done better, achieved more, made me prouder of him than I ever have been in my life? If there were any way to get rid of that stallion – get him hundreds of miles away from here – turn him over to someone else – but who would buy him or accept him as a gift? He's no use to anyone."

Rob knocked the ashes out of his pipe, slipped it in his pocket, stamped across the kitchen to the porch and started to get himself into his outdoor rig. Woollen trousers into overshoes. Canvas trousers over both, tied at the ankles. Sheepskin lined lumberjack, felt-lined gloves, and deep, padded Scotch winter cap. With his hand on the door-knob, he paused and looked back at Nell.

"I would be smart," he said slowly, "to put a bullet through him and haul him away. Ken would never know but what he was still up there in that valley."

Nell made no answer and waited for Rob to open the door and leave. But he did not leave. She looked up finally and saw that he was looking at her, waiting. There was a certain expression on his face. He was suffering. He was furious. He was stumped. He saw only one way out – he didn't want to hurt her, through Ken. He was asking her, and waiting for her answer.

Her heart gave a terrible leap, and she felt weak, and sat down at the table. He was serious about this, and he had put it up to her. She leaned her head on her hands.

Not to judge this like a sentimental woman – to judge it fairly like a judge. No, like someone who has the real responsibility and whose duty it is to find the safest way out for everybody. She could see the years stretch ahead, the constant annoyance and expense to Rob of having these wild mares and their colts brought down for feed and shelter in storms. At last they would feel that the ranch belonged to them. Thunderhead was oriented to

112

this place, there was no way to prevent his coming, except by a sustained programme of discouragement and unkindness that Rob would not be capable of, to say nothing of Ken. And lastly, the worst thing of all, it was only a matter of time before Thunderhead would kill Banner.

A deep wave of compassion for Rob went over her. What terrible decisions he had to take on himself! And such a decision as this – to shoot one of the finest young animals they had ever raised!

Help him! *Comfort* him! She rose swiftly to her feet with outstretched hands. Her face was strong and bright and smiling. "Shoot him now, Rob, and haul him away, before anything terrible happens. We just won't say anything to Ken about it. And don't feel too badly, dear, he's had a glorious life!"

Rob was bewildered. He took her gently in his arms and kissed her, looking at her wonderingly. "Will you go to bed now, my darling, and leave the dishes to me? I'll do them when I come in."

"Oh, you'll be so late – and after all that struggling to sort out the mares! I can do them! I'm not tired!"

"Please, Nell. I'll feel better if I know you're in bed up there with a book. Is there plenty of wood and coal in your box?"

"Plenty. All right, Rob, if it'll make you feel any better, I will."

Nell went to bed and sat reading, but she didn't know what the words meant, for she was listening for a shot. At last she fell asleep, and Rob came in and undressed and put out the lights without waking her.

But there had been no shot, for Rob had thought of another way – just a chance of a way – a very slim chance.

In the morning the storm was still raging. Rob rose early, saddled Shorty and rode over to the telegraph sta-

113

tion to discover the state of the weather and roads westward. It was worst right here on Sherman Hill but snow-ploughs were keeping the highways open and buses were running. Fifty miles to the west no snow was falling.

He rode back and explained his idea to Nell. If he could take Thunderhead in the trailer to Saginaw Falls – if he could make the trip in two days, they would arrive on October twenty-third, the day before the Greenway race. There was still time. And if Thunderhead should give a good account of himself in the race, someone would buy him and take him far away and everybody would be happy. After all, this was what he had been trained for.

"But the storm, Rob! And the roads! And those awful passes! Taking a horse down the Divide in a trailer in such weather as this! "

"Fifty miles west it's clear weather," said Rob as he threw things into his suitcase. "And, Nell – the kid deserves it. The hardest part will be getting out to the highway over the ranch road. It's up to my waist in drifts."

Gus had orders to take Shorty and spend all day, if necessary, driving those wild mares and their colts off the ranch. They would hang around for a while, but with Thunderhead gone, they would be at loose ends, and once off the ranch they would go straight back to their valley and stay there.

Thunderhead was blanketed and put in the trailer, his head tied low so that he would be helpless in case he wanted to make a bolt for freedom.

Big Joe and Tommy were hitched to the home-made snow-plough, and Gus, bundled up like an Eskimo, with only a slit of storm-reddened face visible between cap and collar, forced the horses through the drifts. The car and trailer followed close behind.

114

Chapter Forty-two

Lights blazed out suddenly in the dark room, and Ken began to dream that his father was standing underneath the bright chandelier of the old-fashioned hotel bedroom, talking to Charley Sargent.

They talked about Thunderhead. Again and again Charley said, "I'll be damned." It seemed so real that Ken began to tell himself that it must be true, but still he was asleep and dreaming and unable to drag himself out of the dream.

Then his father said, Don't wake him, and Ken turned to say, I'm awake! and to sit up, but instead he fell deeper into the dream, and presently it faded out entirely and he went sliding down into thick darkness.

It was just beginning to be light when he suddenly sat

up. All night long the dream had been at the edge of his consciousness – was it really a dream? Charley Sargent was, as usual, snoring softly in the twin bed beside him. But Ken wasn't surprised to make out the form of someone else sleeping on the sofa across the room. It was his father.

Ken sat staring, while thought and speculations raced through his mind. What did it mean! Could it mean – was it possible . . .

He slid out of bed noiselessly and began to dress. It was barely a ten minutes' walk from hotel to the stables. Ken made it on the run.

As he saw the long lines of the stables against the faint morning light the suspense was almost unbearable. Running along under the portico of the stable in which Sargent's horses were kept, his eyes probed every dark opening, met the eyes of the quiet, brooding horses.

Long before he reached the last stall, the head of the horse standing in it had been turned in his direction. Ken's sharp thudding footsteps were as familiar as the squeak of the handle of the Goose Bar oat bucket.

A deep grunting murmur surged up through Thunderhead's chest, and the next moment the boy's arms were around his neck.

Presently Ken swung open the door and went in and closed it behind him.

Thunderhead had taught Ken to keep his distance. He had invited fondling from no one but Nell. But now, when Ken put his hands on each side of his face, the big stallion leaned forward and dropped the weight of his head against Ken.

Ken's cheeks burned as he laid them against the satin smoothness of the horse's hide. His hands ran up between the wide dark eyes, playing with the forelock, as he had often played with Flicka's. His lips whispered over and

116

over again, "Thunderhead! Thunderhead!" and then, "You came back!"

Ken moved around him, smoothing his arched neck, tossing the mane to the right side – the proper side for Thunderhead to wear it. He ran his hand and arm down the great muscular ridges. He was filled with the secret joy and astonishment a man might feel when a desired woman suddenly turns and leans upon him. To have won the horse's love after a struggle of years – and such a horse!

Thunderhead suddenly swung his head, and nearly knocked Ken over. There was affection in the nudge – but something else too. Thunderhead wanted to get to the door. Shoving past Ken he reached his head out, pricked his ears, fastened his eyes on the farthest line of the horizon.

His wide nostrils flared and drew in the fresh morning air. They trembled as if struggling to find on the wind some other scent. And suddenly there was a movement, a turn towards Ken, a lowering and swinging of his head, a constriction of his chest that was like an inaudible neigh, and a pang shot through the boy. If Thunderhead had been able to talk, he could not more clearly have said to him, "Where are they all? Who has taken them away? You were there with me, you know that valley and those mares! We were together. Where have you hidden them? If we are friends, you will do this for me – you will give me back my mares! To whom else could I turn?"

Ken, stricken, stood back against the wall, and the stallion restlessly stepped around the stall, switching his tail, came up to Ken, gave him another shove with his nose, again reached his head out of the door and watched the eastern horizon where it was brightening with the morning light. He was tense and quivering all over.

The early-morning activity around the stables was beginning. Little fires were made and breakfast pots began to steam over them. Horses were fed, and brought out by stable boys for washing and grooming. Exercise boys trotted off on ponies, leading racehorses for a slow gallop around the track.

Ken was not alone with his horse long. Perry Gunston and Tommy Pratt came to look him over and give him his morning oats, and presently others of the stablemen and trainers who had heard of the stallion gathered around. Thunderhead would not touch his oats. He nosed them, then turned his head away, standing inert and indifferent.

Gunston was disturbed. "Off his feed?" he said, looking questioningly at Ken.

Ken took some oats in his hand and held them cupped under Thunderhead's soft black muzzle. Thunderhead played with the grains, nuzzled Ken's hand, blew some of them away, then in a weary sort of manner, swung his head aside and stood quietly – waiting.

The boys began to chatter. "It's the trip upset him. When Dusky Maid was brought from Denver, she was off her feed for a week," "He might be coming down with shipping fever." To Ken, "You won't enter him, will you? If he's off his feed like this?"

"It doesn't mean he's out of condition," said Ken scornfully. "He's never out of condition. He can run faster than any other horse any time he wants to."

Gunston suggested that Ken should give the horse a run. He might be willing to eat after he'd had a bit of exercise. Dickson came running up, anxious to inspect the racer he was to ride that afternoon.

"Maybe Dickson had better ride him," suggested Ken to Guston, "so he can get used to him."

But Gunston decided that Ken had better take him

118

out for his first run. They saddled the horse, and Ken mounted him and moved slowly off towards the track. Dickson close beside Ken, and Gunston and Pratt following.

The jockey was firing questions at Ken. Ken answered quietly. No, he doesn't mind the whip. Sometimes you got to beat hell out of him. . . . No, he's not hard-mouthed. You can guide him without any rein at all. He knows where you want to go. . . . Sure, he's got a chance to win the purse . . . he *can* win it, if he wants to, there just isn't any doubt about it. He can run faster than any other horse, I tell you. It's just if he wants to . . . Well – if he takes a notion . . . if he's in a bad temper . . . if he's got anything else on his mind –

As he said the last words, Ken looked uneasily off at the horizon. Dickson looked anxiously at the horse.

Ken added, "Sometimes he starts bad. Don't worry about that. He might start with a rough, hard gallop. That's not his real running gait. Just beat hell out of him. Fight him. Make him mind you. He can catch up with anything once he hits his gait."

When Ken moved out to the track, there was a small crowd strung along the rail, several of them holding stop watches in their hands.

But this was not one of the times when Thunderhead "started bad". The familiarity of the light figure on his back, the well-loved voice, and those feather hands – Thunderhead went from an easy canter without a hitch into his extraordinary floating run, and Perry Gunston's narrow, tense eyes narrowed still more. He glanced at the watch in his hand, looked at Dickson, shook his head, and put the watch away.

Dickson exploded. "Ker-r-rist! You don't *see* a horse run like that! You just dream about it!"

"Gosh Awmighty!" exclaimed one of the others, "he's

got the Greenway purse in his pocket!"

"Looks like Ken's sold his horse," said Gunston.

Further down the rail old Mr. Greenway himself was out watching the morning runs. With his heavy knobbed cane assisting him in keeping his weight off his gouty left foot, and one ear studded with an acousticon like a small black *boutonniere*, he stood with that ear turned towards the track as if by sound as well as sight he could take the measure of these runners. He knew that one of them would be his before night. He was curious to know which one.

It was not until Ken sat down for breakfast with his father in the grill room of the Club House that he learned all the details of Thunderhead's return. It seemed to him more dreadful even than he had thought. The stallion had not just come home alone, as he often had before, he had returned with the entire band of mares and colts – his most cherished possessions – and had trustfully put them in the keeping of the Goose Bar corrals. And now, if his own plans went through, and his father's plans, Thunderhead would never see his mares again.

With head bent down and eyes on his plate, Ken fiddled with his fried eggs.

"Where do you think they all went – the mares and colts?" he asked after a moment.

"Back to their valley," said Rob. "That's their home. They would drift back there – and –" he broke off.

"And –?" prompted Ken, raising his eyes.

"I was going to say," said Rob, "wait for Thunderhead. They'd be expecting him to come back, of course, and take care of them. Why aren't you eating your breakfast?"

Ken ceased all pretence, laid his fork down and leaned back. It was rather a garbled speech that poured out – about Thunderhead's new affection for him. His trust.

And the way he was so terribly lonely for his mares and his valley, and right now when, for the first time, the horse had accepted him and turned towards him as if he was a friend – right now, Ken was playing the part of an enemy to him – not a friend at all.

Rob listened with an impassive face, eating his hearty breakfast with zest, buttering his toast, filling his cup with more hot coffee, glancing around the room, his head cocked as if he was hearing all that was going on as well as the words that came hesitatingly from Ken.

He flashed one lightning glance at his boy. He saw the shadowed eyes, and the pallor and the thin drawn lips that had become familiar signs of Ken's heartache.

Finally he said sharply, "You've been moving heaven and earth for three years to make a racer out of this horse and now you're changing your mind. Can't you stay put? Why in hell do you have to wobble about like that?"

Ken thought that if his father could only see the pictures that moved slowly behind each other in his own mind, he wouldn't ask such things. Right now Ken was seeing the picture of the way Thunderhead had – so trustingly – laid his head against him and placed his whole misery and longing in Ken's hands to straighten out for him.

Ken spoke hesitatingly. "I guess it's just – what you always say yourself, Dad – what we do to horses when we make them do what *we* want, instead of what they were naturally meant to do."

A flashing glance of Rob's fierce blue eyes paid tribute to Ken for this sign of understanding and honesty. "All the same, Ken, we're committed to this and we can't turn back. Neither can Thunderhead turn back. It's too late. Remember, too, how much depends on this."

"What?"

"Have you forgotten all the things you were going to get for your mother?"

Ken winced.

"Right now, with hospital expenses facing us, believe me, if there's any money in Thunderhead, we need it."

Ken's mind began to turn and twist, looking in every direction for some escape for Thunderhead. Touch And Go had run in two races and had not shown in either, although she had nearly been in the money in the second race. She had one more chance, in the race which would follow the Greenway race that afternoon. But certainly she was nothing to count on now.

"And," went on Rob, "remember the things you were going to do for the ranch. Wooden fences. Clear off the debts."

"I know."

"Are you going to turn tail and be a quitter now at the last moment just because Thunderhead is mooning for his mares?"

"But Dad – it's just because – well, he never was like this to me before. He always stared at me, and did things to me, aimed a kick or bite at me, you know. I always had to watch him. But he's changed. He was *glad* to see me this morning – *glad*! He – he –"

"What did he do?"

"Well, he just put his head in my arms and leaned against me the way he always did with Mother, as if I was the only friend he had in the world – and gave a kind of little mumbling grunt, you know the sound, as if it comes right out of his heart."

Rob was silent and could not raise his eyes to look at his boy.

At last he said, "Ken, you've got a divided loyalty here. And there's nothing tougher than that. Whichever way you turn you hurt yourself and someone else too. This happens to people often and it'll be a good experience for you. Are you going to stick to your plan to make money for the ranch and for all our needs – your own too, don't forget that – the money that's needed for your education and Howard's – are you going to carry on with what you've started – what we've all worked for for three years? Or are you going to – well, not exactly quit, but be deflected from your aim at the last moment?"

"Would that be wrong, Dad?"

"It would not be strong, Ken. I could not admire such behaviour. It wouldn't be manly. Sometimes, in life, you have to choose a course that is right and pursue it even if it hurts some innocent party."

Ken did not answer. Rob finished his breakfast, laid down knife and fork and pushed his plate away. "When Dickson gets on that horse this afternoon I want you to be pulling for them both with all your heart and soul."

Ken's face began to burn. Visualizing Thunderhead prancing out with Dickson on his back, he couldn't do anything *but* pull for him! The idea of any other horse beating Thunderhead!

"And remember this, Ken, although right now Thunderhead's got his mind on other things than racing, and he's sulking, yet he's been trained for a racehorse. It's in his blood now. And after a little of it, this life will become his true life."

Ken's eyes lifted to his father's with a deep probing question. "Honestly, Dad? As much as his wild life would be?"

Rob hedged. "Well, Ken, you know how I feel about horses. I always regret taking them from their true and natural and self-sufficient lives. But those would not always be necessarily *better* lives, in terms of the horses' well-being and happiness."

This made Ken thoughtful. Rob was getting impatient. He called the waiter and paid the check. A glance at Ken showed him that the boy was still in a state of indecision.

He leaned across the table.

"Listen!"

Ken looked up. There was a different tone in his father's voice and a different look on his face.

"You're going to make your decision right now, Ken, and then stick to it."

"Me?"

"Yes. Be a man. It's your horse. If you want him taken away from the racecourse without making a try, why, it's up to you!"

"Is it, really, Dad?"

"Sure it is." But there was a sharp, contemptuous look in Rob's eyes. "Make your choice!" He leaned back and took out his pipe and lit it, then looked around as if he had no further interest in the subject.

The decision leaped up in Ken, ready-made. He said, suddenly, "He'll run. And he'll win."

The words went through Rob like the twang of a string and caused him the emotion he always felt when one of his boys took a stride towards manhood.

His hand came down on Ken's arm and squeezed it. The other hand reached for his hat. "Come on, son! We'll go out and see to getting Thunderhead's shoes changed."

They walked out to the stables together, and if anything more had been necessary to crystallize Ken's determination, it was the remark his father made as they reached Thunderhead's stall. "Of course, Ken, if he doesn't win, and if we have to take him back, you realize I can't have him around the ranch any more. I'll have to sell him for anything I can get – and that means gelding him first."

Ken came to a dead stop. "But Dad! I'd get him off the ranch. He'd go back to his valley!"

"But he wouldn't stay," said Rob simply, "and sooner or later he'd get in a fight with Banner – and, well – you know what that means. You saw –"

Chapter Forty-three

Thunderhead did not like Dickson, and came out of the stall fighting.

The rest of the field were off and away on the two-mile race while Dickson was still trying to shake the bit out of Thunderhead's teeth and head him in the right direction.

The ordinary, run-of-the-mill excitement of racetracks which flares up, climaxes, and dies with every race that is run, is as nothing to the excitement that is generated when something really out of the ordinary happens; when the horses – one or more of them – take the game into their own hands, disregard the plans made for them by man, and stage a show all of their own devising. Then you really see such movement in the grandstands that you think of a river bursting its dam.

As when, at Hialeah in 1933 the two bay mares, Merryweather and Driftway, who had a feud of several years standing, proved the exception to the rule that mares never fight; and threw their jockeys and fought it out, biting, squealing and lashing each other all the way down the home stretch.

As when Dinkybird of the Hawthorne stables took a fall at Jamaica, got up and was mounted again by his jockey, but started running in the wrong direction and could not be stopped.

It was this kind of excitement that Thunderhead of the Goose Bar stables provided for the onlookers at Saginaw Falls on the afternoon of October twenty-fourth.

Ken, standing close against the fence in front of the grandstand, leaned down and thrust his head between the bars. The blood came up into his face as he saw the fight Thunderhead was putting up. The field was way ahead already, Staghorn and Bravura, the two likeliest winners, running in the lead, five others bunched against the rail behind them, and three outclassed contenders trailing hopelessly. Thunderhead stood in the same place, whirling and plunging. Dickson lashed him unmercifully, and, as always, the fury engendered in the horse by this conflict mounted and finally exploded, releasing him from the complex of his inhibitions and flinging him into his smooth running gait.

Ken straightened up, drenched in the sweat of relief. But the field was already sweeping around the turn into the back stretch. The grandstand fell into a sudden breath-holding silence as the white stallion hit his pace, running, as it always seemed with Thunderhead, in the air, propelled by one lightning-quick hoof-thrust after

126

the other, the unbelievable power of which kept him hurtling forward at a speed which was rapidly diminishing the distance between himself and the rest of the field.

Dickson rode with mouth open and a look of dumb amazement, and as Ken glanced around him, he saw this expression mirrored on a hundred faces.

The horses swept around the track.

Thunderhead passed the tail-enders, gradually overtook the next group and at the head of the home stretch passed them too. At that, the grandstand came out of its stupor and a low, sustained sound burst from it. Thunderhead was pulling up on the leaders, then was abreast of them, then passed them. At this, the grandstand rose, swayed and burst into a roar, fluttering hands and programmes and hats.

Thunderhead wavered, and stopped, his flaring, white-ringed eyes and sharply pricked ears turned nervously to this strange heaving mountain to the right of him. At Dickson's yell and the shaking of the bit in his mouth, the stallion went up onto his hind legs.

Bravura and Staghorn rushed past, beginning the second lap of the race.

"Whip him, Dickson! Beat hell out of him!" Ken's voice, cracking with strain, reached Dickson from the crowd. Dickson cast one hopeless glance towards Ken as Thunderhead whirled and plunged, and a wave of the jockey's empty right hand showed that he had lost his whip.

Ken's open mouth closed without another sound and his face paled. Dickson pulled off his cap and beat it from side to side on Thunderhead's neck. Other horses passed him, steaming along the rail. Suddenly Thunderhead plunged forward, and again Ken was weak with relief. He unclenched his fingers slowly. Little bleeding scars were in the palms of his hands. It was all right now –

Thunderhead had passed them once, he could do it again.

But Thunderhead had no intention of doing it. All he wanted, apparently, was a good spot in which to show everyone what he was going to do to this rider whom he didn't want on his back. Angling across the empty track he floated over the inner rail, galloped to the centre, leaped into the air, corkscrewing, came down with feet like four steel pistons – rocked a couple of times, and had no need to do more. For Dickson was making one of those slow curves through the air that Ken had made, times without number.

Free of his rider, Thunderhead decided to join the race. He floated over the rail again – and the beautiful easy leap drew a gasp from the grandstand – and then he started to overtake the field. Again it grew like an orchestral crescendo – the roar of the grandstand – until the white horse closed the distance between himself and the rest of the field.

Thunderhead did not know when to stop. He floated on when the race was over and the winner proclaimed and the other horses were walking back into the paddock. Attendants ran out on the track and tried to stop him. That angered him. He dodged them, sailed over the outer rail and ways into the distance, the little stirrups dangling and tapping at his sides.

When Thunderhead vanished beyond the grove of willows south of the race track, Ken fought through the crowd behind him, under the grandstand out at the back and around the west end of the track. He ran as fast as he could, keeping his eye on that little dip in the willows through which Thunderhead had disappeared.

He felt in his pocket. The whistle was there. If he could get within earshot of the stallion he could call him with the whistle. He fought his way through a dense patch of

128

undergrowth, emerged, and stood for a moment searching the country before him, his scarlet face streaming with sweat, the wild mop of his hair tangled with bits of leaves and bark.

Half-a-mile away the white stallion stood quietly. When Ken whistled for him, he turned his head, then trotted towards his young master.

As he came up, Ken looked at him bitterly. "You fool! You've thrown away the only chance you had in the world!"

Thunderhead stopped, recognizing something other than approval in Ken's voice.

"You *could* have done it! Easy as pie! And now you've spoiled everything!" There was a tremor in Ken's voice as he finished, and he said nothing more, but mounted the horse and rode him slowly back, circling the track to reach the stables.

As he did so, he heard by the roar from the grandstand that another race was in progress, and drew rein on a little elevation and turned in the saddle just in time to see the horses flash over the finish line – a bright golden sorrel with blonde tail a good length in the lead.

Touch And Go! He had entirely forgotten that she was running! And now she had won! A flood of joy alternated with the feeling that it could not possibly be true.

Ken galloped Thunderhead to the stables, not dismounting to open gates, but jumping every one. He put the stallion in his stall, called to one of the stable boys to attend to him, and ran back to the race track.

He was in time to hear the announcement over the loudspeaker. "Winner, Touch And Go, of the Goose Bar stables. Owner, Kenneth McLaughlin."

Ken stood still a moment. This was what victory felt like – then he dashed forward. He wanted to get his hands on Touch And Go and see if she was really still herself.

Perry Gunston had her in the paddock. A blanket had been thrown over her, and around her was a crowd of men. Rob McLaughlin was talking to old Mr. Greenway, and he called Ken to him and said, "I want you to meet Mr. Greenway. This is my son, Mr. Greenway, the owner and trainer of the filly."

As Ken put out his hand he heard an eager little whinney behind him.

Mr. Greenway exclaimed, "You don't say! You don't say! And I hear you trained the white stallion too. But you'll never have any luck with him, my boy, too un-dependable."

The whinney came again and Ken longed to go to her.

"Mr. Greenway has just bought Touch And Go, Ken."

"Bought her!"

"I'm a collector of fine horses, my boy. That's the second one I've acquired this afternoon. Hop up on her now, son, and ride her over to my stables."

Mr. Greenway limped over to the filly. Rob caught Ken's arm and showed him the cheque. It was made out to Kenneth McLaughlin, and the amount was five thousand dollars.

Ken looked up at his father. Rob McLaughlin's big white teeth were flashing in a wide and joyful grin. "That does it, Ken!" he exclaimed. But Ken could only stare at his father's face, then at the cheque, and feel dazed.

Greenway called to Ken, "Take a last ride on her, son."

Touch And Go's face was turned eagerly toward Ken as he walked to her. A sudden reluctance made his feet heavy – *last ride!*

He smoothed her face. His father and Greenway stood

130

beside her, talking. "Good girl," murmured Ken, "you did it, baby."

It was a marvel, certainly, what she had done. Without any fuss about it, she had just always done as she was taught to do and done it with all her heart. And she had it in her, that speed and power, as if she had been Flicka – Flicka with the four beautiful legs she had had before he, Ken McLaughlin, had brought her in off the range and lamed her – but, too, with the sweetness and docility that she had only acquired through her suffering.

"Good girl," he muttered again, and turned his face down against the filly's head that was gently shoving at him. Then he put it into Swedish, "my *flicka* –"

Perry Gunston drew the blanket off, Ken mounted her and rode her slowly toward the Greenway stables.

"Are you awake, Thunderhead?" It was a soft whisper from Ken who had spent the night on a blanket at the edge of Thunderhead's stall.

The stallion did not move. He was standing with his head out the upper half of the stable door. But one ear flicked back and Ken rose to his feet and went to the door and folded his arms over the top of it close by Thunderhead's neck. Outside, the light grew stronger. It was nearly day.

Ken thought over all that had happened and all that was going to happen. He and his father and Thunderhead were starting back to the ranch this day. Then Thunderhead would be gelded – plenty of money now to have Doc Hicks come to the ranch to do it – and then he would be sold to the Army for a band horse. They brought the most money of all, his father had said, more than the Army paid for ordinary horses. He might bring as much as three hundred dollars. White horses for cavalry bands were not easy to find.

Ken stared out at the dim shapes of stables and trees

while he thought of Thunderhead carrying a bandsman in a band. He had seen those bands in the parades at the Post. Thunderhead was a big husky – he might carry the kettledrums.

Kettledrums! Cavalry bands! The drummer's arms and big sticks weaving a criss-cross over Thunderhead's back – pounding the drum – putting on a clown act. And the huge glittering horns, the fancy uniforms, the smart drum major, the deafening blare of band music! Thunderhead – the big show-off – prancing in the middle of it!

Ken thought suddenly of getting on Thunderhead and running away with him. Turning him loose somewhere. Giving him away . . .

When they were getting ready to load the stallion, Ken asked, "Dad, is the reason you've got to geld him because you can't get rid of him unless you do?"

"Bright boy!" said Rob sarcastically. Then he put his hand on Ken's shoulder. "It's not the money, Ken – not any more, although three hundred dollars isn't to be sneezed at. But it's really because there's no other way to save Banner and to save myself, incidentally, from having to adopt about thirty wild mares."

Before eight o'clock they had the stallion in the trailer and had started the long drive back to the ranch.

Chapter Forty-four

The eagle headed into the strong westerly wind and hung on motionless wings high over the valley.

The "easterner" had blown itself out and no sign of it remained except for patches of snow under the trees and in the depressions of the hills. Here was summer again. Indian summer, with the quakin'-asp a riot of crimson and ochre and the cottonwoods shedding golden leaves on the surface of the river.

The eagle saw the mares and colts grazing, saw something large and white moving through the pass in the rampart and slipped sideways to poise himself directly over it.

Ken McLaughlin was leading his stallion through the keyhole. As they emerged on the threshold of the valley they halted. The horse was saddled with the small horse-hair saddle Ken had made himself. Underneath the bridle was a heavy chain halter and lead, and over his eyes a blindfold, but in spite of this he knew where he was and his body was tense, and fierce snorting breaths came from his nostrils.

He pawed the earth.

With one hand Ken uncinched the girth, lifted the saddle off and dropped it on the ground. The glint of the sun on steel stirrups struck the eagle's eyes, and a sudden lift of his body registered the reaction. Again he spread his wings wide, circled and centred over the pass.

Ken undid the latch of the throat strap, talking softly to his horse. "You don't know it, Thunderhead . . . but this is good-bye . . . you've got to go to your mares and take care of them and live a stallion's life . . . you're a true throwback, Thunderhead . . . you're not a racehorse though you can go like the wind when you want to . . . and you're not an Army band horse prancing around carrying a kettledrum . . . you've got to go back . . . and I've got to go to school and do a lot of other things . . . so . . . we . . . can't be together any more . . ."

Thunderhead's hoof dug impatiently at the earth. Ken slid his arm up underneath the stallion's neck and laid his own hand against it. His voice went on while his fingers drew off the bridle, the chain halter, and at last the blindfold. "Don't forget me, Thunderhead . . . I won't forget you . . . never, Thunderhead . . ."

Ken stepped back, the stallion was free, and he knew it. He took a step forward, switching his tail. His head was high, his ears alert, his eyes roved over the valley. It was as if he counted every mare and colt grazing there a quarter-mile or so away. But he seemed in no hurry to join them. They were all his, and now there was no one to dispute him.

134

He turned towards Ken again, poked out his head and gave the boy an affectionate shove. Ken slipped his arm around the stallion's nose. "But you've got to go, Thunderhead . . those are your mares . . . I think you do know it's good-bye . . ."

Thunderhead lifted his head and again examined the mares. Ken tossed the bridle and halter on the ground; and as he did so something that came plummeting down from the sky startled him and made him look up. It levelled off and curved upward again but the shadow of the broad wings slid across the pass and Ken was surprised to see the stallion give a violent start and then half-crouch.

"Why, Thunderhead!" he exclaimed and put out his hand to reassure him.

But the recoil was only for a second. Thunderhead straightened up and threw back his head, snorting out that hated scent.

The eagle circled and came at them again, this time lower, leaning back, his one talon thrust out and his great wings humped forward to break his speed. Thunderhead leaped to meet him, reared to his full height, and delivered half-a-dozen furious pawing strokes.

The eagle slid over them, just out of reach, leaned into the wind again, and a few lazy wing-beats sent him spiralling upward. It was as if he served notice that he was the guardian of the pass and had something to say about this valley. Would it be Thunderhead who would get the eagle under his feet and cut him to pieces, or the eagle who would swoop down to pick the stallion's bones?

This encounter had attracted the attention of the mares. There came trotting out from the band the black mare with the white colt, her ears pricked inquiringly at Thunderhead. She neighed. He answered. He left Ken and went to meet her, lowering his head, curving and

135

wagging it from side to side. His tail lifted, flared wide, and streamed behind him. And now all the mares were staring. They recognized him and rushed to meet him.

The little white colt was the first to reach Thunderhead. It sniffed him, bared its little teeth and nibbled at him in affection, then whirled and thumped him with its heels. This, while Thunderhead and the mare were greeting each other ardently, pressing their faces together, nuzzling each other, finally rising lightly on their hind legs to embrace each other.

Now Thunderhead greeted the rest of his harem. They milled around him, licking and nipping each other in the excited jealousy of having him back. Finally they settled down to the real business of life, which was grazing.

Ken watched it all with a smile on his face. At last he picked up the equipment he had dropped on the ground and went back through the keyhole to finish his business. He had spent hours with drill and sledge-hammer working on the rock around the underneath of that monster boulder which formed the roof of the keyhole. He had studied where each stick of dynamite should go. He did not intend that there would be a single one of those small slips or miscalculations which brought so many of his good intentions to nought. The dynamite was tamped into the holes, the fuses attached.

Now he lit the fuses, turned and ran. He didn't stop running until he reached the place he had picketed Flicka. He slipped his arm up underneath her head and held it against him so she would not be startled, and, standing so, waited for the explosion.

It came. The pile of boulders around and above the keyhole rose with a dull boom. The earth under Ken's feet seemed to heave. There was a frightened chattering of birds, and small animals scurried out of the rocks. A cloud of dust floated up from the passage. And as earth and rocks settled back again, the valley was filled with detonations caroming back from the hills. Last of all came a deep rumble from the Thunderer.

After some minutes Ken entered the passage to see exactly what had happened to the keyhole. It no longer existed. Just as he had planned, the support of the boulder had been blasted away, and with its fall, all the other boulders had found a new position. There were some crannies a cat or small dog could have crawled through, but for Thunderhead the passage was closed for all time.

Ken retraced his steps, ran along under the rampart until he came to the place Thunderhead had made the trail to the summit, and climbed up.

There was excitement amongst the mares over the blasting. Thunderhead was nowhere to be seen. Ken lay down, hanging his head over the edge, certain that the horse was below there, pawing at those stones, investigating every cranny, discovering that there would be no more in and out of the valley. At least, thought Ken, not from this end. You might be able to find a way out the other end, old fellow, through those valleys and mountain passes and glaciers, but it would be a hundred miles around for you to get home, and all of it strange going – no – I think you'll stay in . . .

And then it was as if his father's fiery commanding eyes were suddenly looking into his, and he spoke to them, "I've done it, Dad. He won't come back to bother you any more. Or to kill Banner . . ."

His father! It was a warm and happy thing to remember how his father had looked at him and spoken to him and squeezed his shoulder even at that moment of disturbance getting ready to take his mother to the hospital. And the friendly words, "If you think you can do it, son, I'll leave it to you. I don't want to shoot your horse or geld him." And his mother had slipped her arm around

137

his neck and kissed him and said, "Keep your fingers crossed, darling, we want a little *flicka*, don't we? And Ken – thanks to you and Touch And Go, I'm going away without the slightest worry about expenses – and I shall send out from the hospital and order a new *négligé*! Velvet! With feathers!"

Thunderhead came out from under the rampart at a gallop and rushed back to his mares. Ken leaped to his feet. What would he do now? What did he think about the blocked passage?

Thunderhead was heading away from this end of the valley as if that gunpowder were behind him. He began to round up his mares.

Ken watched it for the last time ... the weaving in and out, the snaking head, the plunges of the mares as they felt the stallion's teeth in their haunches ...

The daylight was fading. Ken had to strain his eyes to see how every mare and colt was gathered up and swept into that rushing charge of pounding bodies and sweeping hair and flying limbs.

Wild exultation filled the boy. He had done it, after all! He had given back the mares to his horse! And this round-up! And a thousand others like it – and the valley and the snow-peaks and the river ...

That other life he had tried to give Thunderhead – the life of a racehorse – how desperately he had prayed for it! He felt almost bewildered. For all his prayers had been denied and all his efforts frustrated, and yet this – *this* – was the answer.

The boy's head lifted and his eyes flashed from crest to crest.

All the world was beginning to glow with the sunset. Three cream-coloured antelopes were drinking at the edge of the river. The river was emerald green and tur-quoise blue and rose pink and there was a big golden star

138

in it. Yellow light swept eastward from the sunset in long level shafts. A half-moon, lying on its back, began to glow like a lamp.

All this for Thunderhead!

Thunderhead floated past the band of mares that now, in the gathering darkness, seemed like a swift-moving blot of shadow, and took the lead.

Ken strained his eyes to see the last of that rushing white form. Here it was, now, the parting. He put up his hand and brushed warm tears from his cheeks, surprised to find them there, because, in spite of the loneliness and the sense of bitter loss, it was as if the beauty of the valley and the gloriousness of Thunderhead's freedom were inside him too.

And now they were gone.

In the deep breath that Ken drew, there was the wideness and the emptiness of the world.

With startling suddenness, day fled from the valley. The golden spears were withdrawn, the pink clouds faded. Shadows seemed to rise from the earth, and, floating on this sea of darkness, the encircling snow peaks turned to ghostly silver. The ice-blue slopes of the Thunderer, marked with triangles and bars of deeper blue, glittered here and there as if strung with diamonds. Its jagged outline lay as sharp as crystal against the emerald sky.

It was time, and more than time, for Ken to go. Flicka was waiting. Once again it was just himself and Flicka, as it had been before Thunderhead, before Touch And Go. He ran down the trail, packed up, mounted, and was off.

The eagle hung in the sky where the daylight still lingered, watching all that the boy did. When he had gone, the great bird dropped slowly down over that pile of boulders which had suddenly changed its shape.

He hovered, examining, estimating the difference. At

139

last he swept up into the sky again, and his harsh, lonely cry, "Kark! – Kark! – Kark!" floated out on the sound waves that played across the valley, spending themselves in inaudible ripples against the mountain-sides.

―――――――――――――

GREEN GRASS OF WYOMING

Thunderhead has returned to the wilds, and poor Ken McLaughlin's hopes of turning him into a world-beating racehorse appear to be at an end.

But . . . Thunderhead comes back! The story of Flicka and Thunderhead continues in *Green Grass of Wyoming*. Again there are three parts, so do look out for Part I. The story rises to a new height of suspense and excitement. You must not miss it!

———————————

DRAGON BOOKS

The Dragon series is one of the finest Children's Libraries in print today. Enid Blyton, Lewis Carroll, Lady Antonia Fraser, Noel Streatfeild, Christine Pullein-Thompson, Mary O'Hara, show-jumper Pat Smythe and many others are all here to delight every child, whatever the mood or time of day. The Dragon authors represent a charming array of the most creative and time-honoured talents ever at work in the children's field – a pasture of absorbing and intimate pleasure through which wind our chequered Pied Pipers with their ageless tunes and tales, to the joy of millions of Dragon readers. As for Kid's Power – Dragon Books are just the thing to occupy young people finding out perhaps for the first time that peace and quiet can be lovely with a book, and who are beginning to discover for themselves the surprising fun in store for them in the world beyond the family.

If you or your parents have trouble in obtaining titles, please remember that they are available from Cash Sales Dept., P.O. Box 11, Falmouth, Cornwall, at the price shown plus 7p postage.

ENID BLYTON (cont.)

Fifteen-Minute Tales   20p
Twenty-Minute Tales   20p
More Twenty-Minute Tales   20p
Eight O'Clock Tales   20p
The Children's Life of Christ   17p
The Red Storybook   20p
The Yellow Storybook   20p
The Blue Storybook   20p
The Green Storybook   20p
Tales from the Bible   17p

MARY O'HARA

My Friend Flicka – Part 1   20p
My Friend Flicka – Part 2   20p
Thunderhead – Part 2   12p
Thunderhead – Part 3   12p
Green Grass of Wyoming – Part 1   12p
Green Grass of Wyoming – Part 2   12p
Green Grass of Wyoming – Part 3   12p

CHRISTINE PULLEIN-THOMPSON

The Open Gate   17p
The Empty Field   17p
The First Rosette   17p
The Second Mount   17p
The Pony Dopers   12p
For Want of a Saddle   20p
The Impossible Horse   20p

MOLLIE CLARKE
(In Colour)

Rabbit and Fox *and* Skillywidden   25p
Mink and the Fire
and Aldar the Trickster   25p

PAT SMYTHE

A Swiss Adventure   20p
A Spanish Adventure   20p

ANTONIA FRASER

King Arthur and the Knights of the
   Round Table (Illus. by Rebecca
   Fraser)   40p

LEWIS CARROLL

Alice's Adventures in Wonderland
   (Original illus.)   25p
Alice's Adventures Through the
   Looking-Glass (Original illus.)   25p

ARTHUR C. CLARKE
Dolphin Island   12p

NOEL STREATFEILD
The House in Cornwall   17p

. . . and many, many more. Enquire at your local bookshop.